Monk Dawson

Piers Paul Read was born in 1941, brought up in Yorkshire and educated at Ampleforth and Cambridge. He spent two years in Germany, one in America and travelled extensively in the Far East and South America.

His other novels are *Polonaise, Game in Heaven with Tussy Marx, The Junkers, The Professor's Daughter* and *The Upstart*. He is also the author of *Alive: The Story of the Andes Survivors* (available in Pan).

Piers Paul Read lives in Yorkshire with his wife and two children.

Piers Paul Read

Monk Dawson

Pan Books London and Sydney

First published 1969 by Martin Secker & Warburg Limited
This edition published 1978 by Pan Books Ltd,
Cavaye Place, London SW10 9PG
© Piers Paul Read 1969
ISBN 0 330 25476 6
Printed and bound in Great Britain by
Richard Clay (The Chaucer Press) Ltd, Bungay, Suffolk

Monk Dawson

One

Acting on mistaken principles of piety and snobbery, my parents sent me to a boarding-school in the English country-side which was run by Benedictine monks. On the first day of the first term they drove me there themselves, to the country house surrounded by woods which smelt of wild garlic and dead crows. I was then seven years old. We were given tea by the headmaster, Father Francis Ashe, in a part of the school that was afterwards out of bounds to the boys, and then they drove away, leaving me alone for the first time in my life—alone with this priest in his black habit and hood.

He was about to take me in when another car drew up on the gravel in front of us. A second family presented itself—a father, a mother and a son of my age. Father Francis turned to meet them and I waited at a respectful distance. The man was tall: the woman seemed like my own mother and for a moment I wanted to rush into her arms . . . but did not. I eyed the other boy and he looked back at me. He was like his father—thin, dark, with brown eyes and black hair.

'This is Eddie,' the mother said to the headmaster.

'I feel sure he should be called Edward now,' said the father.

'Oh no, dear,' said the mother. 'He's always been called Eddie.'

'It doesn't really matter,' said Father Francis in his dry voice. 'Here he will be called Dawson.'

We had beds at different ends of the dormitory and desks at different sides of the classroom because his name was Dawson while mine, Winterman, came towards the end of the alphabet. Nevertheless, because we had arrived together we became friends. In the first crisis of that miserable life he came to my assistance, teaching me how to do up a tie with-out scoffing at me for not knowing. Later I got into a gang with some other boys, but I still saw Dawson on and off and really thought of him as my best friend—a friend who was somehow too precious for everyday use.

One Sunday, about a month after we arrived, we went for a walk together up the avenue which ran from the house to the home farm. The trees that had once lined it had been cut down during the war and the wide margins of grass had been enclosed for the grazing of cattle. I was smaller than he was and could not quite keep up, but did not want to ask him to slow down. He must have noticed my difficulty but rather than laugh at me for my plumpness, he stopped for a mo-ment by a gate into a field. There were five or six black bullocks on the other side which turned and stared at us.

'Are they cows?' Dawson asked me.

'Of course not,' I said with the authority of someone who had been brought up in the country.

'They've no horns.'

'Bulls have horns.'

'What's the difference between bulls and these?'

'Bulls are fathers. Bullocks are just for meat.'

He was silent and remained by the gate, staring into the docile, bulging eyes of the steers. Their gaze was gentle and affectionate.

'They can't have them . . . just to kill them.'

'Yes. For beef and things.'

The air was cold and damp and the afternoon grew darker. He remained staring at the gate, staring at the animals.

'Come on,' I said.

He turned to look at me. There were tears in his eyes which I pretended not to see. I too had cried, but only at night under my blankets.

That evening, for supper, we were given steak-and-kidney

pudding and Dawson refused to eat it. Father Giles who sat at our table told him that he had to finish what he was given but though he ate the potatoes and cabbage, he would not touch the meat.

The headmaster, Father Francis, rang the bell. We all stood and said grace: 'we give thee thanks almighty God for these and all thy benefits which we have received through thy bounty through Christ Our Lord, Amen.' Then, as Father Francis walked out of the refectory, Father Giles called him to our table and showed him Dawson's uneaten steak-and-kidney pudding. This man, normally remote among the senior boys, was now in front of Dawson, and of me, who sat near him. He had sucked-in cheeks and hairs grew out of his nose.

'Eat it,' Father Francis said.

Dawson stood still. His face was bright red.

'Eat it,' the monk repeated, growing red in the face himself. But Dawson would not move. The other boys started shuffling around and whispering. 'Come to my room,' Father Francis said to Dawson, and he walked out.

Dawson was not present at prayers, but he was in bed when we came up. Talking was not allowed in the dormitories so I could not ask him what had happened, but his eyes were red from crying so I guessed that he had been beaten. Next morning he told me that he had had the slipper, which was worse than the stick because it was on the bottom, not on the hands: he had it again that night and the night after until, after three days, he choked down a sausage roll we were given at lunch-time. The next day would have been a Friday.

Across the valley from this preparatory school was the monastery of Kirkham and the upper school to which we were both to go when we were older. I would sometimes stand there with Dawson, discussing what it would be like for us there. 'Oh, we'll really learn how to do things when we get there,' he said. 'Not stupid Latin and all that.'

'What sort of things?'

'Things we can do when we're grown up.'

'I'm going to be a farmer,' I said. 'Will I learn about that?'

'Yes, I should think so. They'll have to teach it if that's what you want to be.'

'What are you going to be?' I asked.

He looked into my eyes, as if to judge how I would receive what he might say. I looked serious and he started to stutter what must have been a secret. 'I'm going to help people,' he said.

'How?'

'I don't know yet,' he said, 'but there are lots of ways. I could be an explorer or invent a medicine or something like that.'

'Everyone wants to do that.'

'I know,' he said, 'but I'm going to, I know it. I'm going to help everyone in the world.'

I left him there, thinking to himself, and went back to fighting, teasing, learning Latin and being beaten. Dawson kept out of fights though he was tall and could have stood up to anyone his own age. He kept to himself and had no friend closer to him than I was. He might have been teased for being bad at games but no one did because he could be sharp with words, saying things that made you look stupid in front of the others though he only did this when he was provoked. Otherwise he was known to be kind and in a way respected for it but not liked, since fighting and nastiness were more fun.

In our third year at the school Dawson's father died. I did not discover until later that he had killed himself. He had been a surgeon in York, a specialist in ear, nose and throat, and no one found out why he did it, but it was this event, I am sure, that gave the monks their early hold over Dawson. He was away for ten days in the middle of term. Father Francis and Father Giles were more circumspect with him when he came back and every now and then he would be called into Father Francis's room, not for the slipper but for a friendly talk. He told me that on these occasions Father Francis always called him Eddie.

Though Dawson never had me to stay in his home, he gave me a good idea of what it was like. His mother was a Catholic because her mother had been half-Italian and so, of course, a Catholic: the father's father had been an Anglican clergyman and his side of the family had provided clergymen, doctors and civil servants to the nation or the East India Company for many generations. No one knew, as I have said, why Mr Dawson killed himself. A sure sign of his normality was the paying of three or four hundred pounds a year to give his son a good education. After his death the holy monks of Kirkham allowed the son to attend their schools for what the widow could afford, which was fixed at half the regular fee. But to meet even this modest expense Mrs Dawson had to live as cheaply as she could and send her daughter to the local grammar school. She was less bitter about it, I am sure, when she remembered that not only was her son taught well, but that his school friends must necessarily be of the kind to be useful to him later in life. Mrs Dawson knew, as we all know, that the sons of the rich go on to become the rich of their day and that the rich not only have their money, but the power that goes with it. So if, by some unfortunate quirk of unpredictable genetics, her son did not have the talents of his father, he would have the friends and acquaintances to fix him up with something respectable, rather than see him sink in society to the level of a plumber or a factory hand.

At the age of thirteen we returned from our summer holidays to the other side of the valley. Dawson and I were put into the same house: they were called after the British Dominions and ours was India. There were several new boys from other schools or straight from home, but life was much the same as before—lessons, prayers, bullying, beating and sport. We now knew enough about the school to expect nothing more though here there was, besides rugby and cricket, the Officers' Training Corps. On Mondays and Fridays the monks themselves would change out of their black habits into military uniforms, and then teach us how best to use bayonets and Bren guns.

Our house-master, adjutant in this little army, was called Father Timothy. We were less in terror of him than we had been of Father Francis and were allowed to call him Father Tim. He himself had been to the school of Kirkham and had passed straight from the school into the monastery, taking the vows of poverty, chastity and obedience and so dedicating his life to God. When we came into his care he was forty-three years old. He smoked a pipe, and cigars when he could get hold of them, so his study smelt of tobacco—a personal smell —as well as polish—a smell general to the school and monastery. His shoes were cleaned for him by the kitchen maids and the mattress on his bed was softer than the pallets on ours. His hair still covered his head. He walked slowly, which may have been from holy insight into the futility of haste. Unlike Father Francis, this monk's face was plump and there were no hairs protruding from his nose, nor much of a growth on his jowls—though he was said to shave and the monastery was known to reject vocations where a vow of chastity would be superfluous. Anyway, his voice was deep, though he liked to talk in a near whisper, except at mass in the morning when he turned to say *Orate Fratres* or *Dominus Vobiscum* when he shouted because most of us had gone back to sleep.

On Thursday evenings he would sit down in the common room with the whole house and talk for a short time on matters of moral and practical guidance. On the first Thursday he talked of responsibility, of how we were doubly privileged in receiving a superior education and in being blessed with the One True Faith: but the greater the privilege, the greater the responsibility we should bear for the state of own souls and the spiritual welfare of our fellow country-men. For some days after this talk, Dawson was more silent than usual. Then one evening after supper he took me aside and asked me how I thought we could do later in life to live up to his responsibility.

'I don't know,' I said. 'I'm going to be a journalist, I think.'

'Is that enough?' he asked. 'I mean . . . do journalists help a lot of people?'

I shrugged my shoulders and then the bell rang for prayers.

The school and monastery were built in different styles and stones, all ugly, but the valley before it was always beautiful—especially in the autumn when a shallow mist clung to the ground beneath the brown trees and the sun shone above it. Gradually, as we grew older, we became aware that there were other elements in the valley, as in the world at large, that had been there for more than the hundred years since the monastery was founded: which had been there before Saint Benedict, before Christ, perhaps before Adam, when the melting glacier, the last remnant of the ice age, had burst through the soft clay to the sea. There were square-edged chips of limestone, fossils of snails and fish. There were oak trees and willows and in summer a heavy growth of elder-berry and nettle. There was wheat where the farmers had planted it for countless generations, and there were cows and sheep and insects with no religion at all. And in ourselves we felt pleasure in the sun or exhilaration at a ground-frost and the emotions of hatred, affection and indifference which were found among us and all men before popes and bishops, synods and councils: and these, like the dandelion which grew in the paving stones between monastery and abbey church, these infiltrated the community of boys and men.

Edward Dawson, now aged sixteen, already with a man's body. He remained taller than the rest of us and had the same thick, black hair, brown eyes and delicate face as when I had first seen him. It was wide at the top and thin towards the chin, which sometimes gave him the look of a Tartar. His eyebrows were most active in giving expression to what he said: his eyes were brown and they always held steady when looking into those of another. He had long hands and fingers: hair started to grow on his body before it did on those of his contemporaries and his mind too showed the same precocious maturity.

Andrew Furness: a boy of thirteen, a lovely child who probably grew into a handsome man. He had soft, fair hair and a plump, pink face. His nose was small, his eyelashes so long that the lower became enmeshed in the upper when he closed his eyes. These eyes were blue and glanced from a lowered head with respect for us, his elders, and also with humour. His teeth stuck out a little so he lisped. His torso was long, but in correct proportion to the rest of his body for a boy of his age.

The monks were acutely aware of the dangers of pederasty. So obsessed were the authorities with the possibility of sentimental and sensual relationships between boys—a custom that was rampant in most other schools of this kind—that they invented a complex of extra taboos. It was not difficult for them to do this in such a small, enclosed society as the school and monastery of Kirkham and so an atmosphere was created in which a boy could not be seen in normal, friendly conversation with another of a different age. Since attraction of this sort was usually of an older boy for a younger one, it effectively prevented seduction of the latter by the former. Once it was learnt—it is said, through the Confessional—that a boy had done something or other with a fourth-former, the poor youth would immediately be isolated in the school infirmary until his parents could come to take him away. The monks had no clear idea of what it was—a grave sin or a mental aberration—but they knew it was contagious and thought it was incurable.

The attention Dawson began to pay to Furness was never, I am sure, such as to provoke passions of that kind. The feeling was pure: the fondness was for the personality. Dawson and I were both dormitory monitors and Furness was in our charge. Like other new boys who had come directly from home, this child was gay, cheeky and affectionate. It was left to the dormitory monitors above all to teach the habits of discipline and for this we were given all powers over the person short of life and death. We had canes and could use them at our discretion. The opportunities for wrong-doing may not have extended far beyond a badly-made bed or a tap left dripping, but there was sufficient scope within these limits for the senior boys to stamp out spirit and impose order. Here, as elsewhere in the school, there was no privacy: the monitor might inspect each boy's possessions and if he discovered, say, the photographs of his mother and sister, he could hold them up for the derision of the crowd.

Dawson, not understanding his own feelings, found himself exercising his disciplinary prerogatives over Furness more than over other boys. He was charmed by his smile and enjoyed the way he could make it come and go with a favour or a threat. Furness reacted to this attention by playing up to Dawson, and after a time it became a game they could not stop. The child was probably unsure in the new school—and bitterly unhappy as most new boys are—and felt flattered and secure in the older boy's interest. He started to behave as if he was expected to give cause for warning or rebuke; as if an evening without incident was a slight to Dawson. And Dawson, I know, began to look forward to the half-hour between prayers and darkness when he was co-tyrant in a kingdom of twenty and could patronize or terrorize his favourite.

One evening, inevitably, Furness went too far. An owl was sitting in a tree outside the window, hooting at its mate. 'Dawson . . . please,' said Furness, 'could you ask the owl to stop hooting?' I smiled: the other boys burst into laughter.

'Get out and bend over the bed,' said Dawson. Such a course of action was normal after such impudence and I came forward to witness the flogging.

'Oh please, Dawson,' said Furness. 'I didn't mean it, I promise. I just said it as a joke, really I did . . .'

'Come on, get out,' I said.

Furness pushed forward his neatly arranged bedclothes and lifted his legs out over the mattress to put his feet on the floor. Then, still sitting, he looked up at us with an expression of real fear. He had never been beaten before—at least not at this school. 'Please, I really didn't mean to say anything,' he said.

I waited for Dawson to answer this time. 'We all heard,' said Dawson. There was a tremor in his voice too.

Chewing his lips, Furness went to the end of his bed and stood there. 'Bend over the bed,' I said. 'You have to bend over the bed.' Furness turned and pushed his knees against the mattress, leaning forward at a slight angle. The other boys in the dormitory were quiet. 'Bend over,' said Dawson, gently pushing the boy's back forward on to the bed: but as he did so, Furness lost his self-control and started to cry. He fell forward, sobbing into the bedcover, clutching at his pyjama cord lest his trousers fall down. His legs dangled towards the floor: his backside was proffered on the edge—but at this moment, Dawson too lost his self-control. He lifted his hand to strike but then seemed overcome with emotion or excitement. He looked for a moment straight into my eyes, then lowered his hand, put the cane on to the bed and left the room. There were gasps and mutterings from the boys: Furness sobbed on. I told the rest to shut up, whacked Furness three times, and then switched off the lights.

What follows is, like much of this story, my own embroidered reconstruction of events. The next day was 29 June, the feast of Saint Peter and Saint Paul. The day was a holiday and we were allowed to go out on our own with packed lunches—the sixth form on their bicycles, the others on foot. On this occasion, Dawson came with Foxe, Burton and me to the nearest town where we threw away our picnics, ate fish and chips out of newspaper and drank a pint of beer in a pub, which was forbidden. I then wanted to go to the film of *The Dam Busters* and so did Burton and Foxe, but Dawson said he wanted to go back, not because the cinema too was out of bounds, but because it was a hot day and he preferred the idea of a swim at school.

When he was within two miles of Kirkham, he saw a small figure waving to him from a field. He got off his bicycle and waited for the little boy, whom he recognized as Smithers out of our dormitory, to reach him.

'Gosh, Dawson, quick. Furness is stuck in the cave.'

There was an old limestone quarry there with what was called a cave half-way up its face—in reality no more than a shelf in the rock where one was sheltered from sight but had an excellent view. Dawson—all of us—had been there on many occasions to smoke.

'How on earth did he get stuck?'

'He tried to go back the top way.'

Dawson put on an expression of weary responsibility, propped his bike up against the fence and set off over the field towards the quarry. Smithers, either because he was puffed out, or because he did not want to be seen out of bounds, lagged behind by the road.

The face of limestone seemed much smaller to Dawson now, at sixteen, than he remembered it through the sense-perception of a boy of fourteen. It was also much easier to climb, though the rock was liable to crumble. He had to make sure of each foot-hold. He could see Furness a few feet above the cave, standing stockstill, his back to the rock face. The boy was white in the face and had been crying. Dawson placed himself firmly a few feet down, and then asked for his hand. Furness edged his left hand towards Dawson, inch by inch. At last the delicate fingers touched Dawson's hand and Dawson was able to clutch the slim wrist. With this support, Furness could climb down past Dawson to the ledge of the cave—and Dawson followed.

'Thanks,' Furness said and started to cry again. Dawson could see the bulge in the little boy's pocket made by the packet of cigarettes.

They sat in the cave—a damp, saucer-shaped surface and Dawson said: 'Oh do stop crying, for God's sake,' and Furness said: 'Oh, you won't tell, will you? Father Tim is just waiting for an excuse to beat me, I know, I know.'

Dawson put his arm around Furness's shoulder. 'You needn't worry,' he said. Furness turned up his damp eyes, blinked his sodden eyelashes and said: 'Oh, thanks, Dawson'; and his white hand clutched the lapel of the older boy's jacket.

Dawson now had the sweet smell of shampoo in his nostrils which came from the delicate hair touching his nose. His arm was around the boy's small shoulders, his fingers patted his arm and his thumb stroked the damp cheek as the sobbing continued. Dawson's long leg was alongside the fragile, trembling limb: his shoulder carried the weight of a heavy head on a relaxed neck . . . and Dawson was inflated with a stronger emotion than he had ever felt in his life before.

Gently, and certainly unconsciously, one of his hands descended from the shoulders to the waist. The sobbing eased: the boy sighed and buried himself further in his protector's arm. Dawson's spirit was still, but his muscles were restless. The fingers of his hand at the boy's waist moved without direction under the band of the trousers and touched the soft skin of his flank. As for Furness—his sobbing stopped, his breathing quickened, but he did not draw away. The hand . . . but then they both heard the voice of Smithers calling them from below.

After prayers that evening, Dawson asked Father Tim if he could see him and the house-master told him to come down to his study when he was ready for bed. When Dawson came in wearing pyjamas and dressing-gown, Father Tim was smoking his pipe. Dawson sat down in the chair next to the desk at which the priest was sitting. The lights were out in the dormitories.

'How are you, Eddie?' asked Father Tim.

'Sir . . . Father . . . it, there's something that I thought I ought to ask you about . . . you see . . .'

'Just tell me what's on your mind,' said the house-master in his low, quiet voice.

'It's just that . . . well . . . I haven't a best friend, a particular friend in the school.'

'Well, you and Winterman seem to get on quite well.'

'Winter . . . yes, but he has other friends.'

'It's a good thing to have several friends.'

'Yes sir, I know, but now, well, I do feel very fond of someone . . . but . . . it's very difficult . . .'

'Do you feel that he doesn't like you?'

'No, it's not that. At least, it might be, but it's difficult to find out because of the distance, you see.'

'How do you mean . . . distance?'

'Well, you see, sir, I'm in the sixth and he's in the fourth.'

Father Timothy did not move and he did not speak. Since those first weeks when he was in the school he had learnt to guard his words and movements—and many years of monastic life had refined this self-control. None the less, the tone with which he spoke after the silence was tight and aggressive.

'Are you telling me that you have become fond of a boy in the fourth form?'

'Yes, sir, I . . .'

'A younger boy?'

'A boy in the fourth, yes, sir.'

'Who?'

'Who?'

'Yes. What's his name?'

'It's Furness, sir.'

'Ah.'

Silence. Dawson had forgotten what he had come to ask or discuss. He had noticed the change of tone in Father Timothy's voice.

'Eddie . . . what do you mean when you say you have become fond of Furness?'

'Well, I seem to like him.'

'And does he like you?'

'I don't know, sir. There's not much way of telling, since I'm a dormitory monitor, you see . . .'

'I mean, has there been any . . . gesture . . . or act of friendship, say, outside the dormitory?'

'No, sir. I've never spoken to him outside . . . except for yesterday, that is.'

Father Timothy leant forward still further. 'What happened yesterday?'

'I'd rather not say . . .'

'You must.'

'They were . . . it would get them into trouble.'

'No, no, I won't take any . . . I mean . . . for God's sake, what did happen?'

Dawson, frightened, spilt the beans. 'It was just that Furness and Smithers were in the quarry but I didn't see them smoking at all. Furness got stuck and Smithers met me on the road so I climbed up and helped him down.'

Father Timothy leant back in his chair. He sighed and straightened his habit—a little worn, a little greasy. Dawson looked down at his own hands.

'Eddie,' said Father Timothy, 'there are some things you may not quite understand, but this . . . friendship for Furness . . . it is not, it cannot be a good thing. Do you understand?'

'Yes, sir.'

'Do you understand why it is wrong?'

'Not really. I thought it might be, though.'

'Why?'

'I don't know.'

'Can you imagine why it might be wrong? An older boy and a younger boy?'

'No, sir. I thought . . . I thought . . .'

'What?'

'I thought that Saint John was the youngest of the disciples, yet he was the one whom Jesus loved the most.'

'Yes, Eddie, that's true: but it's not the same in a boarding school like this.'

'No. I suppose not.'

'How would you . . . I mean, what form would you like your fondness for Furness to take?'

'I don't know, sir. That's one of the things I wanted to ask you. You see, being a dormitory monitor, it's hard to be natural. I should like to be kind to him, sir, not . . .'

'Not what?'

'Not . . . a dormitory monitor.'

'Would you like to touch him?'

'What?'

'Would you like to touch him? To touch his body?'

'I don't know, sir, I . . .'

'You see, I have to explain this to you. When an older boy becomes fond of a younger one, his wish, even if he doesn't know it, is to misuse the other boy's body.'

'Oh no, sir, I . . .'

'Of course, you wouldn't realize that. They often don't realize it until it's too late. What starts as a gesture of affection, Eddie, can quickly become the groping of lust. You'll find yourself handling his penis. Do you abuse your own?'

'No, sir.'

'Good. I'm glad about that Eddie, because it's a hard habit to break. And I'm glad you came to me with your problem and I don't want you to misunderstand what I'm about to suggest. I think a mild beating would be in order here. It's not meant as a punishment, because I'm satisfied that you've done nothing wrong, but as a reminder to the body that our mind can reply to the feelings it sneaks up on us—and this feeling is from the body, Eddie, you must accept that. A few strokes, and the body will be taught its lesson. Now remember: this is not a punishment, and we needn't go ahead with it if you don't agree to it. But my advice, with the benefit of my long experience, is that it would be the best thing if you really want to resist temptation and avoid sin.'

'Yes, sir . . . I . . . if you think . . .'

Edward Dawson who, above all of us, hated being beaten —not because of the pain but because of the indignity—was too confused to disagree with his house-master's suggestion. He stood up and bent over the arm of the chair as instructed by the priest, his testicles pressing against the cool leather. He was given six strokes of a specially manufactured ferula which left blue and pink marks on his buttocks for weeks afterwards—and though his soul may have been saved that evening, Furness was no better off. Later that year, after a gala performance as a candle-bearer at the high altar of the abbey church, he was abducted and debauched by three sixth-formers from another house.

Two

Those of us who have had a private education—a small but piquant part of the population—like to exaggerate its influence on our characters and often talk as if we had no mothers, fathers, brothers or sisters. We were taught to forget them, perhaps, the more easily to serve commerce and empire abroad. Yet three and a half months of each year were spent at home. Eddie Dawson, for example, went back to York at the end of each term, to the house on the Scarborough road which his mother had kept on after her husband's death. The living-room faced the road and was darkened by the trees which lined it. It was a large house, proper for a surgeon and near to the County Hospital. Dawson had his own room, with no particular decoration but a shelf for his own books. His mother worked for a charitable organization and was out for most of the day. She returned at five and made supper and later liked to watch whatever was on television.

His sister Sally was two years younger than Eddie and had her own friends from the local grammar school. She lived at this time in a world of school gossip, pop records and state exams. Her girl-friends had nothing, as yet, to say to boys; and Eddie certainly had nothing to say to them. Sally brought one or two boys back to the house who wore jeans, leather jackets and greased down their hair. What had they to say to the tall boarding-school boy in tweeds and flannels? And if he had said anything to them, if he had opened his mouth, they would have realized at once that he was different—an unfriendly sound, whatever the meaning of the words. This was England in the 1950s.

His mother must have worried about him on several counts—that he had latent instability of mind, like his father;

that he was not taking full advantage of his private education which had cost her so much; that he was ashamed of her or his home, because he never asked anyone to stay. Of course Dawson was not ashamed of his home, however cheerless and drab it may have been, but he did not envisage friendship whose fruit was constant companionship. He liked to be alone, here as at school to read, to think. He remained in his room much of the time, or walked to the bookshops in Stonegate. The house, quite naturally, had its atmosphere of femininity—but rancid femininity that comes with women who live without men. For example, his mother and sister, during the term, would never bother to cook an elaborate meal: but when Eddie was there one or other would do it, though both found it a nuisance. They did so because they felt they had to: he exerted no authority over either of them.

It is conceivable that Sally was jealous of him not for the sake of his education but for the clothes and records she might have had with some of the money that went to Kirkham. But they were an English family: no thought was ever spoken. They were silent and polite and went their own ways.

Perhaps it is implied that the mother was somehow cold towards her son: but in fact she hugged and kissed him whenever he came home or went away. She talked to him whenever she could think of something to say. She took him to the theatre—once, even, to the Covent Garden Opera which was touring in Leeds. She never mentioned her husband, his father, because she had nothing to say about him. She was a heavy woman and an ordinary one. Her friends were mostly widows or spinsters. She knew few people with children Eddie's age and anyway he seemed happy to be left alone until the day came to go back to school.

Religion was never forced on us at Kirkham: religious instruction was the least important subject on the curriculum, and we all left the school particularly ignorant of the substance of our supposed beliefs. But this was not the product of negligence. The monks of this order of Saint Benedict were only following the tactics of another order, the Society of Jesus. Ten years in a monastic institution could be assumed to have left its mark at a far deeper level than that of mere consciousness. No one could decide to forsake what they had inexorably become. No one could deny his own identity. For years, now, for fourteen years we had been to mass every day of the term, and twice on Sundays. On Thursdays there had been Benediction. On Sunday evenings, Vespers. Every morning there were prayers before classes with the head-master: every evening, prayers before bed with the house-master. God entered into everything we did. No aspect of our lives was without its good or bad, its right or wrong. Faith became as automatic as the habits of hygiene . . . and we thought as little of being Catholics as of brushing our teeth.

That some boys should see more in their religion than this was both expected and encouraged. It happened, quite natur-ally, that during these long periods in church growing minds should ponder and reflect. It was, in fact, the only time when they were left alone. Nothing could stop some of them from thinking of sports or their sisters' friends or of Furness as a candle-bearer: but on Sundays when the monks' voices gently sang the Gradual, or as the boys bellowed the Agnus Dei, it was not unusual for some of us to think of God, of the apostles, the disciples, the saints. As the monks filed into the church before a ceremony, or as the procession moved out afterwards with the great silver crucifix bright beside the candles, the fourth-formers all in white, the tall monks all in black, the novices, the prior, the abbot and finally the cele-brant in his bright robes—as all this happened before our eyes, it was inevitable that some of our minds would be touched by its theatre. Thoughts would surely turn to the highest form of heroism that we had been taught to recognize—the heroism of sanctity. We all knew that most of us would end up as soldiers or business men but each one understood that above all these banal vocations there might be, just possibly, a call from God. It was not made quite clear to us that not all saints are priests and not all calls are to the clergy. It may be that the recruitment problems of the Church do not allow for such frankness and detachment: all armies have used press-gangs, and seminaries in Italy are happy to take boys from the age of eight. How many mothers are in heaven for the sale of their sons?

England, of course, is not Italy and most of my contemporaries at Kirkham went into the laity. However, like a proud regiment the Benedictines did not want to see any of their vocations lost to the Jesuits or the Dominicans, so when a boy's pious ambitions persisted—and the monks were sharp to see the signs—they were gently guided homeward. A call from God was not just a cry from one person to another: it was an administrative question, a yearly routine, a gathering of the crops which had been sown on fertile ground.

'What do you think, sir?' Dawson asked Father Timothy in a private conversation. 'Should I try for Oxford, do you think?'

'Yes, Eddie, you could do that . . . or Cambridge. You should enter for a scholarship too.'

'Isn't it worth thinking of any others?'

'I don't think so, no. Not other universities. Other careers, perhaps . . .'

'What sort of thing?'

'Have you any idea as to what you might do after university?'

'No . . . I'm a bit confused.'

'Do you pray for guidance?'

'Yes, I do. I pray to be given some idea of how I can set about what I feel I'm destined to do.'

'What is that?'

'It . . . well, it sounds so conceited and vague. But I do

feel a desire—no, it's more than that—it's an ambition, really, an ambition to benefit humanity.'

'That's a very fine ambition, Eddie, and there are several ways in which you can try to do that, aren't there? You could become a surgeon like your father.'

'I know, but, well, I can't get away from wanting to do something bigger if you see what I mean. A doctor or a surgeon or a social worker—they can only help people one at a time. I'd like to serve a nation, if you see what I mean, like a great king or a politician . . . but politics is no good these days, is it?'

'Not really . . .'

Dawson smiled, not at the priest but at himself. 'It's silly, isn't it: being sure you're meant to do something but not knowing what it is.'

Father Timothy's eyes wandered to the ceiling. 'You mustn't forget to look under your nose.'

'How do you mean?'

'God's answer may be so obvious that you don't notice it.'

'I . . .'

'After all, why did God make us?'

'Well, to know, love and serve him . . .'

'Exactly. Him. Isn't it for his sake that you wish to benefit your fellow men?'

'Yes, sir, of course . . .'

'And though one can serve him as a surgeon or a stock-broker, there is one, pure way of serving God which is not serving him as anything, but is simply serving him . . .'

'Yes, sir. You mean . . . I had thought of that.'

'It might be the way . . .'

'It's hard to tell.'

'It is indeed.'

There was a moment of silence. Dawson, in the same chair as always, looked at his hands: Father Timothy sat at, and looked at, his desk.

'If it's any help to you,' said the monk, looking up at his pupil, 'I had always thought of you as someone who might have a vocation to be a priest. I have noticed that you often stay behind in chapel.'

'Yes sir . . . you see, I had thought of it, but I can't quite see how it really does benefit other people.'

Dawson's words were cautious but the contorted brow over his face would have shown Father Timothy the anguish behind what he said—if Father Timothy had in fact been looking at Dawson: but he was back to staring at his desk.

'It would be a mistake,' said the priest, 'to get things the wrong way around. You surely want to help others because you feel God wishes you to do so, because Christ commanded us to love our neighbour as ourselves. But remember the story of the young man who came to Christ and said that he had obeyed all his commandments and so what should he do now? And Christ said to him: give all you have to the poor and follow me.'

'How did you know you had a vocation, sir?'

'Me? With me it was very dull. I wanted to be a priest from the age of twelve. But do you know about Father Donald?'

'No.'

'Well, he couldn't make up his mind about his vocation, so he said to God—if I see a spider in the next twenty-four hours, without looking for one in particular, I shall take it as a sign that you are calling me to the priesthood. He said this at six in the evening, and by four the next afternoon he had not seen the spider. Then, at five past five, he took a book from a shelf and one of those very, very small spiders was hanging from it.'

'What was the book?'

'What was the book? I don't know. I don't think that matters, really, does it? Remember, Eddie, God has ordained that his priests be equal to the angels.'

It was towards the end of our last term. Dawson was pre-occupied and I saw less of him than usual, for we were all either worried or excited about leaving the school and going out into the world. He did once ask me what I thought of the idea of joining the monastery.

'What?' I said. 'Join the monastery? You must be mad.'

'Seriously . . . I think I have a vocation.'

'How do you know?'

'I've always had this feeling that I should help other people. You know. We talked about it.'

'Yes, but you used to admire Napoleon . . .'

He looked confused. 'I've grown up a bit since then.'

'Have you grown up completely? Mightn't you change your mind again?'

'I don't think so. I think all that vague feeling of destiny was just leading up to a priest's vocation. As Father Tim says, the best way of serving others is by serving God.'

At that age I could not admit to myself the mild horror I felt at Dawson's own plan for his future. I knew he had seen a lot of Father Tim and suspected that his decision was not entirely his own: but who was I to disagree with a priest, let alone with God.

'Don't you think,' I said, 'that some experience of the world outside Kirkham would give you more understanding and so enrich your vocation? I shouldn't have thought you'd make much of a priest if you went straight from the school into the monastery.'

Dawson seemed impressed with this argument of mine. He then told me of Father Donald and his experiences with the spider and I encouraged him to ask for a sign of this sort. He thus suggested to God that if his pen ran out of ink before the day after next, he would take it as a sign that he was indeed destined for the priesthood. The pen did not run out of ink: but Dawson decided that the nature of the minor miracle was not random nor poetic enough for the attention of his creator. While walking down from India house to the main school, he conceived of the idea of a red rose-tree before Sunday as the necessary sign: but returning to lunch he saw just such a tree growing at the door of the house which, unconsciously, must have given him the idea in the first place.

He went once more to Father Timothy—as usual, late at night when the others were asleep.

'Don't you think,' he asked, 'that I might make a better priest if I had a year or two away from here?'

'You forget, Eddie,' said Father Timothy, 'that I myself came straight from the school into the monastery.'

'I'm sorry, I didn't mean . . .'

'No, no. It's a natural question. But you see, Eddie, a man does not need experience of the world to open his soul to the workings of God's grace. He does not need to know the earth to pray to Heaven. When people talk about experience, these days, they mean compromise—compromise with sin in a world which is the principality of the Devil. I tell you, Eddie, if you went out, you might never be able to come in again.'

Never to come in. Already, in his imagination, Dawson walked the pleasant cloisters and heard the same peaceful bells he had heard since he was a child.

'As often as God calls you,' Father Timothy went on, 'the Devil will block your ears. He will think of all the reasons you could ever want for not dedicating your life to God. All the apparently sensible arguments. Your youth. Your inexperience. When you hear them, Eddie, remember that this is the Devil arguing with you, the Devil trying to shout down God.'

After this there was no dialogue in Dawson's mind and in the summer when the rest of us finally left school, he was received into the monastery, taking the name John after the disciple whom Jesus loved.

Three

Dawson's contemporaries now went out into the world, some into the Army, others to Oxford and Cambridge or straight into business corporations. A few missed their days at Kirkham, others never looked back—but for all of us life changed. For Dawson it went on as before. The first year in the novitiate was as if a seventh form followed the sixth. He proceeded from a curriculum of history and English to one of Latin and Theology. The older monks were his teachers.

There are several steps in the career of a priest—porter, acolyte, sub-deacon, deacon: Dawson reached these and passed them as he had passed from the second eleven to the first eleven in the school cricket teams—and, six years after taking his first vows, he came to take his last and be ordained as a priest. It was, he was told, the greatest moment of his life, and his mother and sister came from York to witness it. I too was invited and drove up from London.

He appeared, among many celebrants and acolytes at the altar, dressed in a long smock of white linen. Then, as the business progressed, a cord was strung around his waist, a band of cloth placed over his left arm and an embroidered strip over his head. After many prayers and much incense, the bishop laid hands upon him and he was then and there a creature equal to the angels.

Together with the bishop and the other three who were ordained with him, Dawson said his first mass 'to God who gives joy to my youth'. They performed their first miracle —'for this is my body'. The round piece of what is called bread but has the appearance of blotting paper, became for them the body of Christ—the contemporary of Tiberius and Seneca the Younger. Dawson believed this to be true and most of those around him believed it to be true. On Dawson's face, and on the faces of the three others, there were dazed and tired expressions: excitement and prayer had surely kept them from sleeping the night before. Their feelings were now solemn, humble and full of love of God. Their parents looked on: in some faces there was pride, in others bafflement.

After the ceremony and a few private prayers of thanksgiving, Dawson came out into the sun. A small crowd of monks and teachers gathered round him to shake his hand and receive the highly potent blessing of the newly ordained priest. They knelt and Dawson gave his blessing, exuding happy confidence in his priestly powers. He embraced his mother and she knelt for a blessing, kissing the hands of her sacred son. His sister knelt too but with a sour expression on her face. And then, from behind, I placed my hand on his shoulder. Dawson turned and smiled into my face. 'I'm so glad you came,' he said. I shook his hand and congratulated him, but did not kneel. I looked into his face to study the changes of six years: there were none. No lines. No shadows. He had grown an inch or two, perhaps, and his slim body had a more angular appearance—but on his handsome, honest face there were no signs of change since our days in the sixth form. He studied me and under his scrutiny I felt for the first time ill-at-ease in my tailor-made suit and pastel shirt. He glanced at the sports car parked casually at the door as if it necessarily belonged to me and betrayed the drinking, indolence and sexual incidents of my life. I felt especially that my attempts at charm were not taken as kindness but hypocrisy—but then suddenly he seemed to change his mind or think of something else. He took me by the arm. 'You are the world,' he said, 'the world for which we work and pray. I think of you often, you know. You are . . . for me . . . a point of concentration for my prayers.'

He was smiling when he spoke. 'I hope you don't feel that I'm interfering . . .'

'On the contrary,' I said, smiling. 'My life has gone so well: it must be your prayers.'

Dawson introduced me to his mother and sister. I could not make much of the girl—unlike her brother, she was plain—but the mother was easy to talk to. I told her about what I had done since I had left the school and she said that she sometimes wished that Eddie had led an ordinary life like that—but of course there was no greater honour than the priesthood and a monk at Kirkham was not at all the same thing as an ordinary parish priest.

No bride was happier at her wedding than Dawson on his ordination day. He blessed and he smiled and he shook hands and all the Community looked on with benign pride—the middle-aged and old in their black habits. Above all, he had witnesses from the world—his sister, his mother, myself. After a while we all moved over to the guest house where there was to be a reception: I stayed for a while, talking to the abbot and Father Timothy, but for some reason I found their company oppressive and so excused myself on the grounds that it was a long drive back to London.

Dawson took on many duties at Kirkham, teaching English and Latin, running the school printing press, the Rhodesia third fifteen. Then, in spring, the boys went home and the school and monastery were immediately quiet. For the first time in six years, Dawson too left the monastery, the valley of Kirkham, taking a train across the country to York. Monks these days, he was told, do not shut out the world or evade their ordinary, human responsibilities. It was known that Mrs Dawson was a widow and that he was her only son. He was therefore advised, even ordered, to visit her in his old home. One can well imagine that he felt strange leaving Kirkham and walking in the streets in his clerical suit of clothes. People react to a priest in very different ways. Some, mostly old women, give them warm, friendly looks while others, both men and women, look at them with expressions of loathing and disgust. This only happened to Dawson once on this occasion: as he entered the railway compartment and settled in an empty seat, a man and a woman rose and left it, taking their luggage down from the rack and giving him just such a look. It left him nauseated for the first half-hour of the journey—but this was the world and it was his duty to face it.

His mother talked a great deal and he sat in the kitchen listening to her, but her conversation was a continuation aloud of an inner monologue and he found it difficult to concentrate on what she said.

'It's funny to think of you as a priest, Eddie, really, though I suppose I shall get used to the idea. A priest's mother is expected to be very proud, isn't she? It's not that I'm not proud. I am. It's so lovely at Kirkham that I can quite see why anyone would want to stay there. I don't know what your father would have thought, though. You're very like him, you know, but then so is Sally. Neither of you have turned out like me. I expect you're both quite relieved about that, though I think I might have made a nun, you know. It must be so peaceful, just praying and singing and teaching those boys—nice boys, aren't they?—they're getting some West Indian children in the grammar school here. The railway workers . . . you know. Some people make a fuss about it but I don't see why, really. They couldn't be worse than some of those boys Sally used to bring home. Though they do say that they have diseases and things which come from Jamaica— and we just don't have the natural immunity to them. But Mrs Jenkins says it's only the kind of disease that spreads if you're married to one, so they'll probably keep it to themselves. . . .

'Do you think the churches will ever join up? It certainly would suit me because most of the other ladies at the Charity are C of E and really in a city like this it's all bound to go through the archbishop at one time or another so it seems rather funny to go to different churches on Sunday. Though I can't imagine priests being married. A clergyman is never the same as a priest to me. I'd never confess to Mrs Pott's husband. Can you imagine being married? It's a pity in a way, of course, but Sally'll probably have children and get married. I'm a little worried about Sally, Eddie, I mean . . . if it's any use worrying about that sort of thing. She doesn't go to church any more, you know. She used to come with me, but last Christmas she came back from Leeds and on Christmas Eve she just said she wasn't going. Well, I told her that I myself couldn't imagine Christmas without midnight mass, but she said she could and she wasn't going, and she can be so sharp, you know, so I left it at that and she hasn't been since, as far as I know. Of course you had a much better education, so you can't blame her, but she'll probably get over it. I dare say it depends a lot on whom she marries in the end. I'm rather afraid that if she marries a Catholic, he'll be an Irishman. There are so many Irish among Catholics, aren't there? that what's so nice about Kirkham—they're all English priests, aren't they? Here we only get Irish ones. Mind you, I like Father MacSweeny . . . he isn't always going on about money, but it's the way they talk that I find so disagreeable. I mean, the Yorkshire accent is rather a nice one, don't you think, but the Irish one . . . I don't like it at all. And they're so stupid. Really, Father MacSweeny has to say some quite ridiculous things to get people to understand the simplest doctrine. . . . There are a lot of Irish in our congregation, you see. Railway workers too, I dare say. . . .

'Now the people in the Minster are a nice lot, but it just isn't church for me. Do you know what I mean? It's more like a museum with all those people going round and no lamp over the altar and no candles or statues of Our Lady. I wouldn't feel at all comfortable at an Anglican service.'

The only fact that Dawson picked out of his mother's

stream-of-consciousness was the information about Sally and the state of her soul. She was at home at the time but kept out of his way. Whenever her eyes met his, they seemed to express slight contempt.

Sally Dawson was not pretty, nor sentimental, nor did she dabble in glamour any more. Her brother had a better face and figure than she did, which could not be ascribed to his expensive education but may not have led her to love him more. Her hair was mouse-brown and straight: her nose was rather too large for her face; her legs too short for her torso. Her face was thin like her brother's, but the father's features which gave him some distinction gave her a certain masculinity. This is not to say that she was unfeminine: but at this age in particular she had reacted from the silliness of her adolescence and had become serious, thoughtful and severe. She never wore scent or cosmetics. She bothered little about her appearance. She hardly spoke to her mother, but shuffled irritatedly around her, snorting with disdain if either of the two others made a remark she considered speculative. In her mother's case, the speculation would be gossip: in her brother's, it would be anything he might say to manoeuvre the mood of the family to godly cheerfulness. She might have made an excellent linguistic philosopher, except that she would have considered it unnecessary, and at Leeds University she studied Physics.

She kept out of the house for most of the day, going to work in the City Library. Father John hovered around the house for a day or two before managing to be alone with her. When he did, it was late at night on the last evening he was to be there. Their mother had gone to bed. Sally, it seemed, always watched television until it went off the air and Dawson decided to watch with her and do his duty as a priest. The film dragged on: Dawson hardly noticed it but prepared his remarks. They were both silent during the commercials and the film, but eventually it came to an end. Sally got to her feet and would have left the room at once but Dawson said to her, 'Sally', and she stopped, reluctantly, and faced him.

'Yes?'

'Sally,' he said. 'You mustn't forget I'm your brother . . . just because I'm a priest.'

'No,' she said, 'I don't.' She did not sit down.

'I would like to ask you, if you don't mind, about how you feel about the Church and our religion and God . . .'

'Oh Eddie, for Christ's sake . . .' she said, and pulling at her roll-on through her jeans, she went up the stairs and slammed the door of her bedroom.

When he returned to Kirkham, the posts for rugby football had been taken down and the cricket pitches had been mown and rolled ready for the boys' return. The short spring of that part of the country had already turned into summer. There were rainy days, but the vegetation grew all the same and the flies came with the leaves on the trees so there was always scent and sound outside the buildings.

Father John Dawson sat in his cool room, his cell, preparing the lessons for the term. Every now and then he looked up from his work, turned around, and thought how fine it was. Here was peace. Here was prayer. Here was a life that was holy because it was simple and dedicated to God . . . even if, at that moment, it was taken up with the conjugation of Latin verbs. He had a bed—a black bed with a thin, horse-hair mattress on which he slept well from ten each night to five each morning. He had two pairs of lace-up black shoes, four sets of underclothes, six pairs of black socks. He had one clerical suit with shirt and dog-collar for travelling and two sets of monks' clothes—one new and one handed down from Father Michael who had died just before he, John, had entered the novitiate. The walls of his room were white. There was a small window which looked out over the valley and on the wall opposite the window there was a large crucifix —black wood with a cream plastic figure of the suffering Saviour.

He had a rudimentary bookcase containing his breviary, some text books, one or two biographies of saints, some poetry—Hopkins—and a volume of the Catholic Encyclopedia. On top of the chest of drawers which contained his clothes there was an ordinary safety razor with the cheapest kind of blade. This blade was expected to last him a week— though some of the older monks with tougher beards were allowed to change their blades more often. Dawson, whose growth was strong, found that the blade pulled and pinched towards the end of the week but in this age when corporal penance was not permitted by the hierarchy, when hair-shirts were forbidden by the rules of the Order, he was glad that there was at least this slight pain to offer joyously to the Lord.

There might have been some other things in the cell— an allowance of cigarettes if he had smoked, some other books of a non-religious nature, a clock inherited from a grandparent or a silver propelling pencil given by a friend—for though the monks of this Community had no private property, nevertheless there was a natural tolerance of certain minimal personal effects. Any human being, even a monk, needs one or two small objects he can call his own, or else like Saint Herbert he is compelled to befriend a beetle or a fly. But it was pleasant for Dawson to know that, beyond these small objects, a man needs nothing; his acquisitive instincts come only with a worldly environment. Here in the monastery, day in, day out, Dawson had no money in his pocket. He sat in clean, rough clothes in this simple, white room. When a bell rang, he went to teach or to pray or to eat: or he stood to say a prayer in his own room—as at the Angelus—knowing that every monk in the community, wherever he might be, was doing the same.

There were small ripples of disruption in this placid pond of holiness—laziness in one monk, a chip on the shoulder of another, or incompatibilities of temperament between a third and a fourth. There were also conflicts with the boys—the idle and the impudent who could play havoc with a priest of too tender a conscience. Such a priest was Father John who was still either remote, or spoke with too sharp a tongue which estranged his pupils.

One afternoon, in the middle of the summer term, Father John Dawson was walking up from a game of cricket for which he had acted as umpire. He saw three boys, half-hidden by a pavilion. Two were of an age to be in the sixth form: the third was two or three years younger, a frail and gentle-looking boy. This younger one was bent over and one of the older boys then kicked him with apparently as much effort as he could put into it. He was wearing heavy cricket boots and tears could be seen on the cheeks of the small boy as Father John approached them.

'What's going on?' he asked.

'Hands in pockets, sir,' one of the sixth-formers replied, referring to the custom whereby a sixth-former could kick a fourth-form boy if the latter was caught with his hands in his trouser pockets.

'Sir, sir,' said the little boy, 'I was just getting a handkerchief out.'

'That's what they all say,' said the sixth-former.

'It's true, I promise,' said the fourth-former.

'Anyway,' said Father John, 'he's been kicked so I suggest you all get back up to your house.'

'We both saw him, sir,' said the second sixth-former, 'so we both get to kick him.'

Father John then lost his sacerdotal reserve. 'I saw you kick him, and it was vicious and dangerous. Now what's your house and who's your house-master?'

The three of them cowered. 'India, sir. Father Timothy.'

'Well, you'll all three report to Father Timothy and he can decide whether this boy should be kicked again or not.'

The two sixth-formers skulked off. Father John walked up to the school with the younger boy. 'Gosh, sir, they're always kicking me. Me and Miller. They always say we've got our hands in our pockets even if we haven't—not even a handkerchief or anything.'

'Why don't you tell Father Timothy about it?'

'Well, I would, sir, I don't know, though . . . it might not do anything, if you see what I mean, and then the others would get to know and that might make it worse. I thought of going to see Ransome because he's head of the house and quite decent, but you can't tell what they'll do, can you?'

'I should have thought you could trust them.'

'Were you in the school, sir?'

'Yes, I was.'

'Oh well, then, you should know. Anyway, we're all going to see Father Timothy now.'

That evening Father John went up to Father Timothy in one of the classroom corridors and asked if he could talk to him. This priest who had been his house-master was too preoccupied with the school to play much part in the monastery: in consequence John had seen little of him in the past six years. With effort, now he spoke to him as to an equal. He told him what he had seen and what he had said. Father Timothy, who had smiled when they had first met, now frowned.

'Yes, John,' he said. 'I know about this. But if you were a house-master you would understand that it is much better to let the boys work out this kind of thing among themselves.'

'Yes, father, I see that. But there seemed to be a real danger of injuring the boy.'

'That is a question for the headmaster—whether this custom should be allowed to continue or not. I've never heard of a boy being injured by it, I must say. As to this incident, it is strictly a matter for me to decide . . .'

'Yes, of course, I had no intention of interfering. It was just that this boy said that he and . . . Miller, I think it was, were always being kicked like this for no reason at all.'

'For no reason . . . That's what they all say. But if it's a case of one boy's word against another's, then a house-master must believe the boy in authority. If I upheld a fourth-former over a sixth-former, then the whole structure of discipline in the house would collapse. There'd be chaos.'

'But if you don't, surely it means, possibly, a toleration of injustice?'

'My dear John, we are training our boys for life in the world, not in some ideal Utopia. Putting up with injustice is one of the most important lessons we can teach them.'

Of course Dawson was a monk before he was a school-teacher and much of his life was spent in devotion. He sang Matins and Vespers and mass with the rest of the Community: and alone studied the life of Christ and the Rule of Saint Benedict. Moreover, he liked to read accounts of his patron, Saint John the Evangelist, and those of other saints called John. There were several of them: John of the Goths and John of the Grating, or the Johns of Matha, Matera and Meda of whom little or nothing was known so little or nothing could be learnt. On the other hand, some of the giants had been called John: John the Baptist who had prepared the way of Christ, or John of the Cross, the mystic doctor of the Church, or the two great saints who had dedicated their lives to the care and education of boys—John Bosco and John Baptist de la Salle. There was John Fisher, the great English saint, and there was John Vianney, the Curé d'Ars, whose special place in the Church was unaffected by the discovery that his patron, Saint Philomena, had never existed.

John—John Dawson—studied these lives to see his own

way to saintliness, for that, of course, was the object of his cenobitical life. He decided, through his own computation, that there could be four different kinds of holiness, four different paths to sanctity. Which was to be his?

The first was through successful administration of the Church—the saintliness of popes such as Saint Gregory, and missionaries such as Saint Patrick. The second was through writing and scholarship—to be a man like Saint Augustine or Saint Thomas Aquinas. The third way was through asceticism, either the mystic variety of Saint John of the Cross, or the self-abnegating mysticism of Saint Francis of Assisi. The fourth and final category of saints were surely those who tried to love their fellow men as themselves, who were as charitable as Christ had commanded them to be, by caring for the poor, the diseased and the uneducated. It was surely in this last category that John should place himself because the work of the community to which he belonged was education.

It came to disturb him, however, that there was no evident link between the virtue of Charity, which had inspired all other saintly educators, and the work which was done at Kirkham. The boys they taught were not orphans or beggars —nor was there any danger that they would receive no education if the monks were not there to provide it. At half-term there was a short holiday: the countryside at once became cluttered with the expensive cars of the boys' parents who came to visit them—sky-blue Jaguars and plum-coloured Rolls-Royces. The sires of his pupils were not scabrous and destitute, but prosperous professionals, businessmen and landowners. Their mothers were not fallen women whose bodies were exploited for sin, but respectable matrons of this or that county or suburb. The proof of all this was the three or four hundred pounds each family found for each of its sons. Where, in God's name, was the charity? In relieving the parents of their proper duty? Was the word of God to be taught in exlusivity to the pampered children of the privileged few?

Dawson went with this question to his confessor, Father Maximilian, one of the kindest and most holy monks in the Community. This priest had been his novice-master and he felt for him entire trust and respect. From the shrivelled face under unruly grey hair had always come the most wise advice. Dawson's sins, of course, had mostly been of a monastic sort —dozing off at Matins, losing patience with a pupil, thinking malicious thoughts about another priest—but Father Maximilian was always able to relate their triviality to the majesty of his vocation.

After confessing his usual batch of transgressions, John posed his question. Father Maximilian buried his face in his hands for a moment and then he answered: 'You are mistaken in thinking of our work here as exclusively charitable . . . in the sense, say, of Saint Francis de Salle's vocation, or that of Saint Vincent de Paul. You see, we live in a non-Catholic country, in a society which becomes less and less Christian. Our vocation is to train certain members of the laity to carry, by their example, the word of Christ into this pagan world. To attest, like the Baptist, to the good news of Christ's coming and his Resurrection.'

Dawson thought about this for a week, and at his next confession he returned to the subject.

'But why, Father,' he asked, 'why do we choose the sons of the rich alone as apostles in the world? Why don't we take the poor? Or the Faithful at random? Or why don't we go out ourselves?'

Father Maximilian pondered again. John could see through the grille the tired, holy face as it pressed into the palms of his hands. Then it re-emerged. 'The reason for that,' said his confessor, 'lies in the traditional tactics of the Church. It is a historical question. You see, there are, and have always been, missionary orders, charitable orders, scholars and mendicants:

but when, at the Reformation, the Church went through one of its greatest crises, it was decided, by the Jesuits, that the best method of preventing the spread of heresy was to foster loyalty to the Church in the leaders of society. In those days, it was the princes and noblemen.'

'Yes.'

'It was, you see, the period of *cujus regio, ejus religio*. Secure the prince, and you have his subjects.'

'And does this still apply?'

'Things are not quite the same,' replied Father Maximilian, 'but this principle remains the justification for our choosing our boys . . . the sons of the rich, as you call them. It's just that these days the principality is the factory and the office and the influence is by example rather than by rule.'

On 9 October 1958, Pope Pius XII died at Castel Gandolfo. The consistory of cardinals met in Rome to choose a successor. The archbishop of Milan was the favourite, but they chose instead Roncalli, later Pope John XXIII. It was not understood at the time, except possibly by the Holy Spirit, what effect this choice would have on the Church. Then Pope John issued a letter to all the Faithful entitled *Mater et Magister*. It became clear at once that this new pontiff had in mind a total reversal of the Catholic Church's traditional attitude on social questions. No longer were the pious permitted to believe that the material plight of their fellow men was irrelevant to the quest for eternal salvation. This logic, which had kept Sicilians starving and South Americans in economic servitude, was destroyed by the Pope's reiteration of Christ's remark: 'I have compassion on the multitude . . .'

Now the Church, though obedient to its Pope, was nevertheless composed of men and women who found it hard to change. No command from Rome could alter their natures: it could only encourage that element among them who found the command to their liking, that which we call liberal and progressive. All over the world, this element took the initiative, using the encyclical against their reactionary bishops. Bavarian prelates said mass in their native German: Dutch pastors turned about and faced their congregation. Catholic priests and Protestant ministers were seen, in Antwerp, to talk to each other ... and in St Louis, Missouri, to hold services together. Laymen took communion in both kinds—they drank the wine as well as ate the bread. The reformist ideas spread from the homelands of Luther and Calvin to France and America. New ideas for new reforms were postulated. John XXIII called a General Council of the Church to meet in the Vatican City. All the bishops and abbots of Christendom came to Rome, and many of the reforms were accepted for the whole Church. The liturgy was shortened, retranslated and pruned of offensive references to Muslims and Jews. Nuns were permitted to modernize their habits: French priests were allowed to wear grey instead of black.

Pope John died. A new pope was elected, and for the moment the movement for reform seemed to lose some of its purity and benevolence. Its inspiration, which had been love, now became expediency—to make the Church of Christ relevant to the modern world. But the modern world was a small part of the entire phenomenon of the human race, and many pious people found themselves passed by in the reforms and so isolated from the Church. Not least the orders. Nuns, who had been encouraged to make themselves pertinent by changing their robes and cowls for contemporary and conventional skirts, in some cases decided that their vocations were as out of place as their veils. Indeed many individual monks and nuns decided that if the life they had led until then was somehow irrelevant, then no reform could help it. And so they left.

The Catholic Church in England was protected from these harsh changes by its easy and insular situation. There was no competition for righteousness as there was, say, in Holland with its vital Protestantism and moral Socialism. There were no Mormons or Baptists hunting for wavering souls, as in the United States. A handful of Dominican friars did their best to ferment discussion and reform, but the large part of the clergy still looked to Dublin rather than to the Continent for inspiration and example—except the English Congregation of Benedictines, which had a tradition all of its own.

Father John Dawson, who had worried so much about his saintliness, might be called a small molecule of the phenomenon of religious turmoil that became so evident all over the world. He was protected from its most rampant manifestations, but he did read the Catholic quarterlies and there came a time when the public press carried stories of the battles between liberal priests and conservative bishops, and of teaching orders of nuns who first feminized and then secularized themselves. And any priest who ran off and got married was sure of a big spread, for though our population practises no kind of religion, it is left with a curiosity about those who try.

When Dawson eventually realized what was happening in the rest of the Universal Church, it unleashed in him a frenzy of reformist zeal. With one or two others among the younger priests, he petitioned the abbot to be allowed to say mass in English. The abbot acquiesced. Then they asked that the Officers' Training Corps be abolished, but since the weekly parades and yearly field days were dear to the hearts of many of the monks, this was only considered.

Dawson's first real victory within the monastery was a painful one. It was the collapse of Father Maximilian, his confessor. Dawson browbeat him, he almost rebuked him, with the papal encyclicals and the deliberations of the Council. He consistently and brutally repeated his doubts about the nature of their work at Kirkham, that it could not be God's will, let alone the intention of Saint Benedict or the apostle

John. Father Maximilian buried his face in his hands for longer and longer periods—he must have had doubts of his own—and eventually begged the abbot for respite. A post was found for him as chaplain to a small but unreformed community of uuns.

The abbot must have been shaken by the collapse of Father Maximilian and he made up his mind to deal with Father John himself. The Holy Spirit had done well to guide the Community to elect this man as abbot: he was only fifty years old, and young in manner—gay, confident—but firm in his authority. The paraclete had certainly concluded that if you cannot have a saint in such a position, you had better have a politician—and this, without doubt, he was, one of the finest, and without even the advantage of being an Irishman. Though the abbot himself liked the idea of reform and thought of himself as a reformer he was sensitive to the feelings of the majority and aware of the structure of the school. Father Timothy, for example, who was neither old nor reactionary, disapproved of reforms which affected the school such as the abolition of the Training Corps. His thesis, which the abbot accepted, was that the nature of the school at Kirkham must be related to English society, not to the Roman Church. Their religion might be as pure and modern as you like, but the businessmen of Birmingham and the aristocracy of Scotland would not send their sons to an academy for saints. Thus the monks continued to teach the boys how to kill, and one or two of the more fanatical reformers were found parishes in South Wales.

Dawson was too young as yet to be sent on such a mission; but the abbot saw his energies and found a mean for their expression. There was, around Kirkham, a parish comprising the maids, gardeners, stokers and labourers who worked in the school, the monastery and the monastery farm. With wives and children, there were more than a hundred and fifty of them. The priest who had care of their souls was brought

48

back to teach mathematics, and Father John was appointed in his place.

Some months before there had arisen a problem in the parish whose solution was to be left to Dawson. A labourer on the monastery farm, Fred Joliff, had absconded, leaving his wife and children and work. This man was himself slow-witted, but his wife was more clinically insane—'daft' was the word used in the village. They were both of that class of rural fool which lives quite happily in a world of beasts and kale, but suffers and deteriorates in a city. Mollie, the wife, was a bastard herself and had had three children before she went to live with Fred Joliff. But then the parish priest, Dawson's predecessor, had persuaded the two to marry, and Mollie had three more children after that.

She was a tall woman, and beautiful in a way, but just as some women will make the most of their qualities with tints and shades and creams, so Mollie made the least of hers. Her bosom had been sucked into such a state that it hung under her dress as a shapeless swelling. Her legs were bumped with protruding veins and her hair was uncombed and greasy. Yet her insanity had freed her from most kinds of anxiety and her face was unusually clear of lines and wrinkles, and her eyes were candid and direct like those of a child.

She had no concept of cleanliness—a result of her madness —and so did not impart any to her children. They were not taught to use the pot, since she had never grasped the art: they were never told to wash their hands and it never occurred to Mollie to wash their clothes. Fred had brought back ten or eleven pounds a week, and the people at the Post Office made sure that she received all the allowance due to her. And of course the family lived rent-free because the cottage went with the job on the farm.

After four years of life with Mollie, leaving the stink of pigs in the evening for the greater stench of his wife and children at home, and a tea of bread and butter, and beans out of a tin, Fred Joliff decided that he could find a better life and so fled the house, the progeny and the situation. No one could tell how far Mollie's feelings were hurt by this: her only reaction was a growing unease for herself and her children. But the problem, in an enlightened society such as ours, was not one of money: the local inspector of the Ministry of Pensions and National Insurance made sure that she had enough of that. The problem was the cottage. The farmer needed it for a new hand. No man would take the job without a cottage. The farmer was a patient man. He presented his problem to the County Council, which returned it to him: there was no vacant Council house at that time. The farmer then widened the problem to one of care and presented it again to the Council. The Council, however, could not take care of the mother and the children together. They had facilities for deserted children and they had a home for incapable adults, but they could not simply provide lodging for a homeless family. Thus tentative efforts were made to separate Mollie from her children: some had said that she would not mind. But when they tried it, they found it physically impossible: sensing their purpose, she clung to all six of the children and later became demented. She roamed the streets of the village with her family, approaching anyone she could find and telling them her story in incoherent half-sentences.

Dawson rushed into this situation with the fervour of a frustrated saint. He castigated the farmer who then lost his patience and shouted him out of the house. He telephoned the local County Councillor and made him tackle the county officials—but they had their regulations and were adamant. The harvest was at hand and farm labour was short: the farmer had found a man but he needed the cottage. He obtained an eviction order. The mother refused to leave the children. The Council refused to take them together. The doctor refused to certify the mother—so Father John took them in hand. He led them out of their cottage, pulling their bedding and pots and pans on a cart. He took them through the village and down three miles of country road to the school and monastery of Kirkham: once there, he led them to the school theatre and behind its stage to the green room. There was there a lavatory, a basin and a small electric ring used for making coffee during rehearsals.

Dawson then saw to it that they had food. He himself washed the children's hands and faces and some of their clothes, all in the same small basin, revelling in the stink. He made up camp beds which he had requisitioned from the Training Corps store-room. He comforted Mollie, un-flinchingly laying his hands on her shoulder, sodden as it was with coagulated sweat which had spread from the under-side. He emptied drawers of Shakespearean costumes and filled them with the few rags of the children's and Mollie's other skirt, crusted as it was with every variety of dirt and exudation.

The other monks were outraged. For one thing, they said, there was the danger of scandal—a woman in the care of a monk. For another, it was interference in the workings of the Welfare State. The situation was worsened by Mollie Joliff's sallies into the school with her six stinking children to explain her plight to any little boy who could be cornered in a classroom or a corridor. The monks would come upon a group of thirty boys whooping and shrieking around an inner circle of Mollie, her brats and an embarrassed but polite pupil whom she was addressing. The monks would sweep her out, which doubled the whoops and shrieks and the crowd of boys. Order might be restored, but classes in that area of the school started a quarter of an hour late.

Father John had not consulted anyone before taking Mollie Joliff to the theatre. The day after, however, he received a message to visit the abbot which he did at once, going to his superior's office, a large room on the ground floor of the monastery. The abbot was dictating letters when he entered, and the novice who acted as his secretary rose and left the room when Dawson came in. The abbot crossed to a sofa and made a gesture to John to sit down next to him.

'You should have asked me, John,' he said.

'I felt it was a task that God had given to me,' Dawson replied.

'That may be so,' said the abbot, 'but you are acting as my representative, you know, in taking care of these souls. The responsibility does not end with you. You never know, I might have come up with some more suitable accommodation for this woman . . . the guest rooms, perhaps.'

Dawson looked up to see if his abbot was mocking him or not but could tell neither from the tone of his voice nor the expression of his face.

'That never occurred to me,' he said.

'There is a danger,' said the abbot, 'of a kind of pride taking hold of our soul when we take charge like that . . . alone. You know, a feeling that only we can do good in this situation.'

'I felt that the Community would have been against the idea.'

'And would their opinion have counted for nothing?'

'The Church . . . I mean, a certain sort of establishment within the Church has always been against . . . against the more positive acts of charity. Saints have usually done good in spite of the Church.'

'Are you a saint, do you think?'

'No, no,' said Dawson, lowering his eyes, 'but I should like to be.'

'Well yes,' said the abbot, 'you're quite right to want to be a saint, but it should be a prayer rather than an ambition, don't you think?'

'It's not ambition, Father, at least I don't think so. It's love, I'm sure it is.'

'Yes,' said the abbot, 'I don't doubt that. But we must all sometimes restrain our love, or else it becomes a blind passion. In this case, you see . . . where does Mrs Joliff go from here —or is she to stay forever in the theatre?'

'No, father . . . something else will be found.'

'It might have been found by now, if she hadn't been brought here.'

'They intended to take her away from her children.'

'They couldn't have done that. It would be against the law, unless Mrs Joliff was certified incapable: and I don't think they'll do that, because then we could ask why it wasn't done before.'

'But she was to have been evicted . . .'

'Quite. That's why they would have had to find her a Council house. Now, as it is, they can say that we have found her somewhere to live, and close their file.'

Dawson looked at the floor and said nothing.

'As a matter of fact,' said the abbot, 'I spoke to Lady Toynton on the telephone this morning and she and her agent are preparing an empty lodge they have there for Mrs Joliff and her children. You might see to it that they get over there: and in future, I think this kind of charity is better left to people like Lady Toynton, don't you? We aren't much good at it.'

Dawson continued his parish work, though a second and older priest was appointed to share the burden. At the same time he went on teaching. He found this more and more tedious, and so his attention wandered, his authority declined and the boys in his class became bored and unruly until each lesson became a trial, too disagreeable, even, to be offered as a sacrifice to God. But Dawson's mind was not subdued. He now became certain that he had been chosen to bring reform to the Community at Kirkham: he was called John as the Pope who had started the movement had been called John.

His companions of the earlier campaigns had all been banished to parishes: he had to work alone. He thus started to engage other monks in conversation about the school—asking them if they really thought that this pampered education for the sons of the rich was a worthy object for a priestly vocation. Was there not a scarcity of priests on the parishes? Were not the missions under strength?

At first his colleagues tried to answer him, but he knew the arguments and could destroy their reasoning with increasing facility. He pursued them until they became confused and embarrassed and tried to avoid him. Some would say there was no more to be said, and would keep their silence, so he took to providing arguments against himself in their presence, goading them with his irony.

'Of course,' he would say, 'how can I have been so short-sighted. Didn't Christ himself say that it is easier for a camel to get through a needle's eye than for a rich man to pass through the gates of Heaven? This, of course, this is why the rich must have the greatest share of spiritual assistance. The poor are blessed anyway. There's no need to bother with them. It's the bankers who need the best priests and the holiest monks. . . .'

There were moments when Dawson would doubt his own mission and feel that this castigation of his fellow monks was malicious and uncharitable. Here, after all, were decent men who had grown up in a tradition where the leaders of society came from the upper and middle classes. Were they sinful because the times had changed more quickly than they had? Perhaps it was the Devil's work to disrupt what they were doing in the school? But was the Devil, then, also behind the Vatican Council which was disrupting much larger areas of the Church? Or was the Devil promoting the conservative element so that the Church would seem yet more alien and quaint to ordinary men and women?

Thus the Devil's side of the question became as real to

Dawson as God's, which was in itself confusing because a reformist trend was to play down the existence of Lucifer, Beelzebub, Satan and Old Nick. But whether they existed or not, Dawson heard a voice which he took to be God's when it advised one thing and the Devil's when it advised another. Then the confusion arose as to which was which.

There were many men in the monastery who might have been thought qualified to distinguish between the voice of God and the voice of the Devil. Unfortunately, as Dawson realized, there was not one without a special interest in which was which. He knew that a conservative would say that one voice was *vox Dei* while a reformist would say it was the other. He would have trusted the decision, perhaps, to Father Maximilian, but Father Maximilian was not there. The only other man to whom he could go was, of course, the abbot himself.

'Father Abbot,' he said, when his audience was granted, 'I realize that I have been a nuisance to you and the Community . . . but I should like to know, how have I done wrong?'

'I have never rebuked you, John,' said the abbot.

'But then . . . if I haven't done wrong . . . have I done right?'

'If you follow your conscience, it is always right.'

'Yes, I know, and that's why I have always argued with the other priests, and have tried to discuss with them the aims of our life here. But now I feel that the voice of my conscience may not be the voice of God, but the voice of the Devil . . . in fact, there is another voice which tells me that I've been slandering the other priests, maliciously suggesting unnecessary doubts. . . .'

'Well, of course,' said the abbot, making a sweep in the air with his right hand, 'when we talk of voices, we don't mean voices, do we? We mean the dialogue that goes on in our mind . . . the workings of our intelligence: judgement, that sort of thing. The two sides of an argument need not have personalities, need they? Let alone those of the Devil and Almighty God?'

'Oh, no, Father Abbot,' said John. 'I know that one of the voices is the voice of the Devil. But to confuse me the Devil makes his voice sound just like God's.'

'Er . . . do you mean . . . you hear . . . voices?' asked the abbot, leaning forward in his chair.

'Yes.'

'Real voices?'

'Voices . . . yes. The voices of God and the Devil, but with no way of knowing which is which.'

'And what do these voices sound like?'

'What do they sound like?'

'Yes. I mean, do they speak English?'

'English. Yes.'

'With any kind of accent?'

'No, not really. They're like yours, or Father Timothy's.'

'You know,' said the abbot, slowly, 'you know that you may be wrong in believing that the voices you hear are those of either God or the Devil. They might just be . . .'

'But Father Abbot,' said John, leaning forward too, 'surely God knows everything? And he allows the Devil to compete for our souls, doesn't he? Isn't the Devil constantly trying to tempt us to do evil? And isn't God always hoping we will resist the temptation with our own free will? I don't see that our vocations would be exempt from this struggle between good and evil. And if it is a matter of moral choice, is it likely that the Devil would leave us alone?'

'A sure method,' said the abbot, twisting his hands together, 'is to pray to God to make his will clear to us, to make the voice of our conscience the only voice. . . .'

Dawson did pray to God and God seemed to answer by shouting louder, but the Devil matched it: and the question of good and evil, of temptation and the resistance of temptation, was carried far beyond questions of Church reform. Such issues as the answering of a boy in class or the eating of a boiled egg at breakfast became a tournament between right and wrong. With all his moral strength and powers of concentration, Dawson struggled with the issues within him, becoming increasingly oblivious to men and matters without. He would be found standing, head bowed, long after the bell had rung for Vespers. Boys in his class would wait embarrassed for twenty minutes while he stood silently in front of them, lost in the recesses of his soul. In the end, one would run off to the headmaster to report the situation. Then, one morning, Father John fainted while saying mass: he had lost much weight, and this ailment of the body gave the abbot of Kirkham the excuse to put him in the monastery's infirmary for the treatment of his mind.

Thanks to God or to the Devil, Dawson's breakdown was shallow and short. The prize fight between right and wrong was stopped in the fifth round, and he was assured by all the monks who visited him that right had won on points. But the abbot did decide in consultation with a psychiatrist, that Father John should not return to the same environment as before.

'It occurred to me, John,' he said, on the first day that the patient was relieved of sedation, 'it occurred to me that while there is no doubt in my mind about the strength and validity of your vocation, there might be some question as to whether this particular Order is best suited to you as a means of serving God.'

'I had thought of that, too,' said Dawson.

'If you will allow me a brief diagnosis of your character, I think you have qualities of great value to a priest. You have love and compassion of a strong and concrete kind which have been frustrated in a monastic life. I think you also have a zeal and an idealism which become uncontrolled and unbalanced in the sort of atmosphere we have here. They need more practical expression to bear fruit.'

'Yes, Father Abbot, I'm sure this is true,' said Dawson, grateful that someone should propose a solution to his troubles.

'Saint Benedict's advice, you remember,' the abbot went on, 'is to temper all things so that the strong may still have something to long for, yet the weak may not draw back in alarm. I'm afraid that there may be more of the weak than the strong here at Kirkham, so we must move ahead slowly. But you are young and strong and out in the parishes there may be something more solid for your enthusiasm.'

'Yes,' said John, 'yes I'm sure . . .'

'You must think about all this,' the abbot said. 'This is your home and you have no obligation to leave it. But if you do feel that the work of a parish priest might fulfil your vocation more than the life of a monk, then I am willing to speak to the Cardinal Archbishop and see if he would not take you into the secular clergy.'

Four

Helen Sweet

London. A girl in her late adolescence sat on the top of a bus which crossed the river Thames on the Vauxhall Bridge. She was short, dark, with stocky legs, dressed in cheap tan-coloured stockings. She wore a tweed skirt and a darned cardigan: on her feet were plastic shoes: between her fingers, a cigarette.

The bus crossed the river. She glanced at the water. The conductor came for the fare and she gave it to him in pennies, having just enough over for the fare back across the bridge.

Her hair was heavy and black: the skin of her face was yellowish, but brown around the eyes. No one noticed her in the street, not even when, as now, she wore lipstick.

At Victoria Station she got off the bus and walked up round by Victoria Street and Ashley Place to the Catholic cathedral. Her eyes glanced up Victoria Street as if, after months south of the river, they had some right to look at the shops: but some resolution had been taken and she passed into the obscure interior of the cathedral.

She walked past the kiosks at the door which offered devotional items for sale—pamphlets, rosaries and medals of the Mother of God. She dipped the fingers of one hand into the bowl of holy water and crossed herself. In the centre of the church she genuflected towards the altar, empty now in the early afternoon. As she stooped she looked up to the roof, high above her, to the level over the coloured marble where the walls were still of darkened brick. It was immense. It was the right place to have come.

At the side of the cathedral there were the smaller chapels, the Stations of the Cross and the plaques to Cardinal Manning and Saint Thomas More. She walked past these until she was behind the pulpit. Here there was the confessional—a wooden hut with three entrances—one for the priest, the other two for the penitents. An orange light was on to show that there was a priest inside. The girl knelt down beside the others who were waiting but she did not examine her conscience because she knew what she was going to say.

Souls were shriven. The line moved forward. The girl waited and then it came to her turn. She went into the confessional and knelt down—pulling the curtain closed behind her. Through the grille she could see the nose of the priest, but his eyes were closed. On the wall to her side there was a crucifix.

'Pray Father give me your blessing for I have sinned.'

The priest said nothing.

'I haven't been to confession since last Easter, Father . . . that's to say, Easter two years ago.'

'Yes . . . ?'

'And since then . . . I've missed mass, sometimes . . .'

'How many times, can you remember?'

'I think about . . . most times, Father.'

'Yes . . .'

'And I've not gone to school on some days, and I've said I was ill when I wasn't.'

'Yes.'

'And I've missed night prayers and I've had nasty thoughts about other people, wishing they'd break their legs and that sort of thing, and I've been rotten to my brothers sometimes though they deserve it most of the time . . . and I've been impure.'

'Is that all?' The priest spoke with a quiet, kind voice.

'Yes.'

'Did this impurity involve anyone else?'

'Yes, Father, a man.'

'And was it a total act of impurity?'

The girl was silent.

'I mean, was it a mortal sin, would you say?'

'Yes, Father, I think so.'

'In fact . . . sexual intercourse?'

'Yes, Father.'

'Has it happened just once?'

'No, Father. Several times.'

'You know that this is a serious sin?'

'Yes, Father.'

'How old are you, my child?'

'Fifteen.'

'Fifteen?'

'Yes, Father.'

'Did you want to commit these acts with this boy?'

'No, Father, not really, and . . .'

'Did he force you?'

'Not exactly, Father, no.'

'Does it occur to you that a moment of selfish pleasure, taken like this, might result in a child with no real parents?'

'Yes, Father.'

'If you just think how much you owe to your own parents . . .'

'M'mother's dead.'

'You've no mother?'

'No, Father, not since I was ten.'

'Do you love this man?'

'No . . . I mean . . . I think . . . I don't know, Father.'

'Do you sleep with him for the pleasure it gives you?'

'Oh no, not really.'

'Do you get pleasure from it?'

'Not really, Father, no.'

'Would you like to marry him?'

'Oh no, Father. I couldn't, you see.'

'I know you're not old enough to marry, but if you felt you

loved him, you could always become engaged.'

'No. Not really. I couldn't.'

'If you don't know if you love him, and you feel you can't ever marry him, then you must try to stop seeing him.'

'I'd like to, Father, but I don't see how not to see him.'

'Couldn't you just tell him that you don't want to see him again?'

'No . . . you see, I can't help seeing him.'

'Is he at your school, or what?'

'No, Father, but he's at home, you see, and there's my two little brothers to look after. I get them to bed but then he comes in from the pub on Friday nights and he drinks that much and I can't really get out from under and there's only the two rooms . . .'

'But surely, if there's a lodger like that, your father . . .'

'It's not a lodger, Father, it's m'Dad, it is, really it is. He won't leave me alone. I tell him to lay off but when he's drunk he won't listen and we've always slept in the same room since m'mother died: and I daren't shout or anything because then the neighbours might wake up and I don't know what they'd say. I try and stop him, Father, really I do, and I'm sorry when he does it because I know we shouldn't, being related like, and I pray to God to stop him because I don't like sinning like that, really I don't.'

The girl got up from her knees, absolved from her sins, and left the confessional. At the same time the priest left the booth from his separate exit, switching off the orange light as he did so. The girl saw him—saw that he was young and tall.

'Would you like some tea?' he asked her.

She nodded her head, obedient rather than thirsty. His hand touched her shoulder and guided her towards the back of the dark cathedral to a door in the blackened brick. They passed through into a hallway at the bottom of a varnished staircase. The priest made a sign to a man who shuffled past them in the obscurity. The air smelt of polish.

With the same gentle impress of his hand on her shoulder, the girl was led by the priest into a small room with three chairs and a table.

'Is this all right?' he asked. 'It's a bit dark, isn't it?' He switched on the light.

'Is it getting late?' the girl asked.

The priest looked at his watch. 'About four.'

'That's fine,' she said. 'I have to be back by six, though, to make tea.'

'Now remember,' said the priest, sitting down and showing her the chair on which she was to sit, 'remember that everything you've said in the Confessional is a secret.'

'Yes, Father.'

'And I won't tell anyone anything.'

'No, Father.'

The priest paused, sighed, and then asked: 'Was your mother a Catholic?'

'Yes, Father.'

'Then you know that I won't tell.'

'Yes, I know you won't.'

'But I think perhaps you ought to tell.'

The girl said nothing.

'I don't even know your name,' the priest said. 'You needn't tell me if you don't want to.'

'Helen.'

'I'm Father Dawson.'

Silence.

'You see, Helen, there are people who could see that you have a room to yourself, away from your father.'

'I have to see to the boys.'

'Yes. You and the boys. It's time you had a room of your own.'

'Yes.'

'And you shouldn't really live with your father if he . . .

well, you know what I mean.'

There was a knock on the door and the porter came in with a tray of tea and teacake. He set it down and left them. The priest poured out the tea. Helen pushed back her brown hair from her face and straightened her neat, thin skirt.

'Would you come with me to see someone like that?' the priest asked.

'Not the coppers.'

'No. Not them. This'd be the Children's Officer . . . Mr Simmonds.'

'An officer's a copper, isn't he?'

'No. Not this one.'

'I couldn't tell him . . . about Dad, I mean.' She tasted the tea: too weak.

'Would you let me tell him? I won't unless you say I can, of course.'

For a moment the girl seemed to sense the man, not the priest—a gorp, a sissy toff. But her eyes came down from his face to the round white collar and black suit. He was not a man: he was a priest.

'Do you think I should?' she asked.

'I think you should.'

'Will they send me away from the boys?'

'Not if you want to stay with them.'

'I look after them, you see. Georgie is only ten and Feddy's not yet thirteen.'

Father Dawson left the room for a while to telephone to Mr Simmonds. He came back and together they left the Victoria Street; he stopped a taxi. They rode together back across the river to the Children's Department of the Borough of Southwark.

Father Dawson came to see her next day to find out how Helen and her two brothers had spent the night in their new lodgings.

'It's very nice,' Helen said, and then she offered him some tea and put the kettle on in the little kitchen that went with this set of rooms. Father Dawson talked to Freddy and George, asking them whether they had made their first Communion. Neither knew what he was talking about.

'It was Mum who took me to church,' Helen said.

'Why didn't she take us?' George asked.

'You were too young, weren't you?' Helen answered.

'I could've gone, couldn't I?' Freddy said.

'Shut up,' said Helen.

Then Freddy and George started to fight and Helen sent them out to the yard. When they had gone and the tea was made, she sat down next to Father Dawson.

'What've they told m'Dad, Father?'

'They've just told him that you're staying here.'

'They're not going to do anything to him, are they?'

'No, I don't think so.'

'Mr Simmonds told me that Dad ought to have got married again. He says it's hard on a working man, not having a wife.'

'Yes, I think he's right.'

'And he says I mustn't think of m'Dad as plain wicked, you see, because there's lots of men who'd act like that if they lived all cramped up, like we were.'

'Did he say that?'

'Yes, Father. And I don't quite understand, you see, because what he did was a sin, wasn't it?'

Father Dawson looked down at his hands and twisted them together. 'It was a sin so far as we know, Helen, but only God can see right into your father's heart and judge just how bad he was to do it.'

'Mr Simmonds says that if we'd had a bigger flat like we ought to have, then m'Dad wouldn't probably have done what he did.'

'No. Perhaps not.'

'Do you think God gave us a small flat to tempt him?'

'I shouldn't think God would do that.'

'Is Mr Simmonds wrong, then, about the flat?'

'No, Helen. Mr Simmonds is a very experienced man. But there are . . . well, different ways of looking at it.'

'But it's true, isn't it, that there ought to be more Council flats, and bigger ones?'

'Yes.'

'And will there be less sins when there are?'

'I don't know, Helen. Only God can tell us that.'

On the Sunday that followed his experiences with Helen Sweet Father Dawson preached at High Mass from the pulpit of the cathedral. His sermon was provocative and abrasive. He told the story, in fictional form, of the girl who was seduced by her father. This in itself was enough to shock the benevolent papas of large Catholic families who sat in tweed suits next to their little girls in pinafore dresses. But the young priest went on to blame this sordid sin on social conditions and the social conditions on the rich and powerful who sat in rows beneath him. He riled the mothers by castigating their expenditure on clothes and then turned on the fathers again, saying that their complacency was just as sinful as the incest of the labourer.

There were several complaints to the archbishop about the grossness of young Father Dawson, but there were more letters of commendation: at last, the archbishop was told, there had been a sermon relevant to the times we live in. Since the archbishop was then preoccupied with this question of relevance, he summoned Father Dawson to see him, warned him of the delicacy of some of their parishioners, but then showed him the congratulatory letters and congratulated him himself. Dawson was told to preach more. It was clearly his strength and talent, provided by God for a purpose.

Thus he was sent out to preach at the many different parishes in the diocese of Westminster—especially in the more fashionable churches of Spanish Place, Cheyne Row and Farm Street. His reputation grew among Catholics and interested non-Catholics. He was allocated a special time and a special place to hear the sins of those who particularly wanted to confess to him.

Five

There came through the grille of Confessional one day the voice of a middle-aged woman that was either affected or foreign, Dawson could not tell which. As he expected she had no particular sins on her conscience but was patently fond of God, her religion and its sacraments. He listened and threw out five decades of the rosary as penance—not to punish her so much as to discourage her and spare his time for the more serious sinners—but even after that, and absolution, she lingered in the Confessional.

'I wonder, Father,' she whispered, 'I wonder if I might ask your advice about something that is not quite to do with my sins but . . .'

'Yes,' he said, thinking to himself that she might be Italian or French.

'It's about my daughter, Father,' she said. 'I wonder if I might persuade you to come to the house sometime to talk to her.'

'Certainly,' said Father Dawson politely, for a priest may never refuse his services, neither to the affected nor to the genteel.

Until Dawson had come to London, when he was twenty-eight, he had only known York, which is one hundred times smaller in size and smaller still in most other respects. Imagine, then, the impression the capital must have made on him—centre that it is for all the pushing, ambitious and picturesque go-getters of the British Commonwealth. There are sights that he had never seen and smells he had never smelt—cooking, women . . . above all the women, for until then Dawson had only known his mother and his sister. In the monastery his thoughts had been elsewhere when other mothers and sisters had come for a week-end to see their little boys. No, to him the female of our species was a category of creature as new and as strange as the giraffes at the Regent's Park zoo.

He had learnt nothing from Sally but now had had a rapid education through the Confessional from little Helen Sweet and others. . . . 'But really, Father, it's so difficult. We used to go out and just kiss but then he'd say he got all sexed up and frustrated and I'd stop him when he'd try to undo my skirt or something like that.' Dawson was at first horrified and then fascinated by what he heard. The Church, after all, had always had such a special place in its heart for the purity of its daughters: virginity was not just a state of experience, but a precious, jewel-studded, gold-encrusted ivory citadel given by God to every female child.

He soon came to see that the owners and inhabitants of these citadels did not seem to value them as highly as they should, and time after time they were surrendered with little struggle on the part of the garrison. Certainly, the armies of chastity were demoralized by the indifference or hostility of those who lived around them. The gold, the ivory and the jewels were somehow out of fashion and, as Dawson himself said to his penitents, there was little use in crying over sacked cities: but even his exhortations to further resistance and counter-attack were reluctantly listened to. If morale seemed high for further encounters, it was often just enthusiasm for a second defeat.

Mrs Carter, the lady who had asked him to tea, had told him in the course of her confession that her marriage was neither happy nor regular. She had no particular sins to confess in that respect: the transgressions were her husband's. It seemed that he loathed her. 'But what can I do?' she asked. 'He was once so loving and so sympathetic towards my faith. Now he never speaks to me: or if he does, it's in such a bitter tone of voice. And whenever I ask what I have done wrong, he just becomes more sarcastic. Really, Father, I'm worried that it's all having a terrible effect on my daughter.'

Her house in Holland Park was tall and elegant, so what the husband denied in conjugal spirit he evidently provided in property. The door, when Dawson went there, was opened by an Italian servant in a white tunic with brass buttons. He was shown into a light drawing-room on the ground floor which looked out on to the square on one side and a garden on the other. The walls of this room were hung with drawings so fine that they were obscure, but whose heavy frames suggested their great value. There were two vases filled with roses and many pieces of bric-à-brac—the stone foot from a Greek or Roman statue, an engraved Arab bowl, an empty but intricate reliquary—all placed on polished, period furniture. In the shelves against the walls there were vellum-bound books and leather albums of photographs with the year embossed in gold.

His hostess, Mrs Carter, came into the room. They both sat down and the Italian servant brought in a tea-tray—silver, porcelain and petit-fours. What a contrast for the eyes and for the nostrils to the Council flats of Lambeth: but Dawson somehow mastered his righteous anger and his face was filled with the muscular forms of solicitous attention as he listened to Mrs Carter express her fears for her daughter's soul.

'Theresa used to be at a boarding-school, you know, but she behaved so badly that the nuns sent her home. She's so shameless, too. She admits that she did it all on purpose so as to be able to live in London. She admits it. Imagine.'

Dawson sipped his tea, smelt the roses and listened.

'I am so worried about her,' she went on. 'Of course her father is an appalling influence—simply appalling—and I often wonder whether she wouldn't be better off without him, but . . . well, as you know, we live in such Godless times and these young people grow up knowing so few good Catholics that they feel they can respect . . . or is that a terrible thing to say?'

'No, not at all. Unfortunately, it's true enough.'

'I would so like it if she could have some Catholic influence in her life that is nothing to do with me. You see, I'm sure she shouldn't feel that Catholicism is me, her mother. What do you think?'

Although she dressed like a grandmother, Mrs Carter had a flirtatious manner and she made a point emphatic by resting her hand on her guest's knee.

'Certainly,' said Dawson, 'if she is going through a normal phase of adolescent rebellion against her parents . . . against you, it would be a pity if this drove her out of the Church.'

'Out of the Church. Exactly. That's just what I'm afraid of. I have a feeling that Theresa only comes to mass to pacify me. Can you imagine that?'

'What is she? Seventeen, eighteen?'

'Seventeen . . . yes.'

'At that age they discover new ideas.'

'Yes, Father, that's just what I thought. If only you could talk to her. You're young and, well, radical. I'm sure she would respect you.'

'Well, she . . .'

'No, I'm sure she would. You're quite different from other priests, aren't you? You're so aware of the social problems, and Theresa is always talking to me about the social problems and I must admit that I don't really understand them. I'm so stupid.' (Hand on knee.)

'I could certainly try to talk to her.'

'Are you sure you have the time, Father? I feel so guilty taking you from the slums and that sort of thing but, after all, we too have souls to be saved.'

'Indeed,' said Dawson.

Later in the afternoon, at about half past five, Dawson saw a girl come up past the window to the front door and he heard the door open and close. Mrs Carter rose and went to the drawing-room door. 'Theresa, dear,' she said, 'would you like to come in for a moment?'

'Well, I can't stay long,' the girl said and entered the drawing-room behind her mother.

She had long brown hair, irregularly cut above her forehead so that, like other girls, she twitched her head every now and then to take it out of her eyes. She had, at this age, a natural grease to her skin which combined with the fine particles of filth in the London air to clot the odd pore and provoke a poisoning of a point of flesh—a blemish that she covered as best she could with pink powdered lotion. She wore a blouse, a belt with a large brass buckle and a skirt so short that Dawson averted his eyes as she sat down.

Her legs, though Dawson did not study them, were then, as later, long but a small measure too sturdy for perfection. In fact her whole frame was large but not graceless. Her eyes were brown like her hair. Her voice was deep and strong with that trace of a croak that is described as richness.

She came into the room swinging a battered leather handbag. Dawson half-rose (a child? a woman?), his hands on the arms of his chair, half-holding his weight: and he intercepted the glance with which Theresa first looked at him, a glance like his sister's—negative alarm, as if setting eyes on a skunk and fearing that it will emit its smell. Then she sat down and looked away.

'Would you like some tea?' her mother asked.

'No thanks. I had some coffee.'

'This is Father Dawson.'

She nodded at him and tossed her hair back and sat slouched in her chair, the chair being the one furthest from the tea-tray.

'Now listen, Theresa,' said Mrs Carter, 'you remember

what you promised.'

'What?'

'That if I let you go to the tutors here, you would have some religious instruction.'

'Honestly, Mum, I don't need it.'

'You promised, darling . . .'

'Okay; okay.'

'Father Dawson has very kindly . . .'

'It's not kindness,' said Dawson, 'it's my job.'

'But we know you have plenty of other things to do.'

'It won't take up much of your time,' said Theresa (impudently), addressing Dawson directly for the first time, but keeping her eyes on the floor.

Whenever Dawson came to see Mrs Carter or Theresa, the husband and father was out of the house. He had a mistress, Theresa told him, and spent most of the time with her.

Theresa was, at first, casual and often rude to her religious instructor. She was in and out of the house six times a day, was often not there at a time they had arranged to meet and she would leave him after five minutes of conversation for some urgent appointment which was likely to be a Western at some circuit cinema. Yet she was quite open and prepared to talk to him when they were alone together. She said that she still believed in God, in Christ, in the Church. There was no doctrine such as Transubstantiation or the Virgin Birth which she doubted: rather her belief was increasingly crowded out of her mind by other more immediate and more urgent pre-occupations.

'I mean, I just think . . . sometimes . . . I think about God. And then I have to run to catch a bus or I see a dress and God's gone.'

'That's why . . . at least it's part of the reason why the Church makes us go to mass on Sundays.'

'I don't think of God at mass. I just think of how bored I am.'

Dawson, aware that she was testing him as much as enquiring of him, gave tolerant answers. 'Yes, well, it's hard to be holy on tap like that. God certainly wants you to enjoy your life,' etc. But Theresa's frivolity led into scepticism. 'I just don't seem to need Faith,' she said, 'and I don't see the need to need it, if you see what I mean. There are so many straightforward, intelligent people who don't believe a word of it, honestly, who think that believing a bit of bread is the body of Jesus Christ is like thinking that babies are brought by storks. I mean . . . goodness . . . Catholics are a type, aren't they? You know, a sort of person all on their own—smug, rightwing—almost a profession, really. And no one seems to know what Catholicism is, these days, anyway. Are we expected to believe in Hell, for instance? I mean, is fear of Hell really meant to be a motivating force in our lives? And what about devils and angels and all that crap? And three hundred day indulgences for saying the right prayer in the right church at the right time, even if your mind's full of the filthiest thoughts. And what about people who aren't Catholics? Buddhists and Muslims and people? I mean . . . to the Chinese and the Africans, Christianity is just colonialism, isn't it? You can't expect them to take the Resurrection seriously if the Missionary's first cousin is busy exploiting them. So they go to Hell, do they, because they heard the word of God and didn't believe in it?'

It became plain to Dawson that as Theresa's intelligence and consciousness of the world grew, it would use what was left of her religion as a punch ball. Though he managed to keep a confident manner with her, he had never before had to face an assault of this kind—doubt charged with the energy of youth. He was also aware that her thoughts were not the quirks of an individual, but the bedrock of generally accepted agnosticism.

'I mean, for God's sake, here's Mum carrying on like a devout Catholic, yet she spends masses of money on Italian servants and clothes and dinner parties. I mean I do think that if you do believe in Christ and all that, you ought at least to do what he says you should do—give all you have to the poor and follow him. Don't you? And if you haven't the guts to do that, you should bloody well shut up.'

Father Dawson could only prevaricate and shrug his shoulders at arguments like that—putting in a few words for human weakness and God's mercy.

One afternoon, late in autumn, they sat drinking tea, in the drawing-room of Theresa's home. The afternoon grew darker: the light in the room became green, but neither bothered to put on the light. They had been talking about Birth Control—Dawson taking the liberal attitude that it was up to an individual's conscience, yet trying, at the same time, to explain the Church's classical teaching. Suddenly Theresa leant forward and asked him, 'How do you manage without sex? Don't you like it, or what?'

'I don't know,' said Dawson. 'I've never had it.'

'But don't you ever wonder what it's like?'

'I think one has some idea. Even Christ had the body of an ordinary man, you know.'

'That's what I don't understand. Well, Christ, that's easy because he was God: but priests. I mean, all the men I know seem to need sex: at least, that's what they say.'

'It would be the line they'd take,' said Dawson, dryly.

'I'm not a virgin, you know.'

(Silence.)

'You didn't have to tell me that,' said Dawson quietly.

Just as quietly, Theresa said, 'Don't you see? That's what's wrong with you and Mum, saying that. With the people I go around with, well, with any of the people my age, it isn't something you tell or don't tell . . . a sort of dirty secret. If

75

you have a boy-friend, you sleep with him. It's taken for granted.'

'Even if you're a Catholic?'

'Yes. Because it would be . . . I don't know . . . what you'd call against my conscience not to sleep with a boy if I loved him.'

'If you loved him, perhaps . . .'

'It's not so difficult. It's the people who are screwed up about sex who cause the most unhappiness. People like my mother.'

'Why her?'

'She and Dad hardly slept with each other after I was conceived, you know, so you can't blame Dad for having a mistress.'

'Why? What went wrong?'

'I used to think it was all Dad's fault, that he treated Mum pretty shittily and all that: but later I saw how cold she was, really. I mean, do you know, every time after they'd slept together she'd get out of bed and on to her knees to say her night prayers?'

'How do you know?'

'Dad told me and I asked Mum and she admitted it. She said she couldn't get to sleep unless she did. She must be frigid, really. It's not her fault. But I don't blame Dad for going off, either. He's been much nicer to me since he did. Being repressed is horrible.'

Dawson was not surprised that Theresa had slept with her boy-friends. He knew from the confessional that if she did she was only conforming to the general pattern of contemporary behaviour. But he did not concede her soul to the Devil: in fact he had not even started a counter-attack and as he planned it he felt that there were elements in favour of his campaign. 'I think you're having such a good effect on Theresa,' Mrs Carter told him. 'She really likes you and respects you and she's stopped seeing that awful boy with a scooter.'

The winter campaign, when it got under way, was not a matter of new arguments for Faith or Chastity. Dawson knew the limits to reason. Rather she should keep her Faith through the process that she had already begun—respect for someone who not only believed, but made religion his life—Father Dawson.

He therefore tried to see more of her. They met for lunch in restaurants. He showed her parts of London she had not seen before—the Thames at Limehouse, the old docks beneath Tower Bridge. He was helped in this strategy by what must have been an act of God: Theresa had been dropped by her boy-friend, the boy with the scooter, and seemed not to care much for the two or three others who sometimes took her out.

Dawson and Theresa Carter talked freely together—about sex, religion, marriage, politics and art. There were conversations in which the priest, disguising his curiosity as fraternal concern, learnt as much about the world and the principality of the Devil as Theresa did about religion and the Kingdom of God.

'I mean . . . you can't say that the values of Victorian England were good ones, can you,' asked Theresa, 'since they meant hypocrisy, violence and terrible materialism. Goodness, Western societies are the most materialistic that have ever existed, aren't they?'

'I think it is difficult to make moral judgements on social movements. You must distinguish between cause and purpose. The crusaders, for instance, are now thought to have been an early manifestation of West European imperialism: but at the time a large number of them really did believe they were doing something good and disinterested. And, you see, a stockbroker like your father may be motivated by a desire to make a lot of money, but his investments do provide work for those who might otherwise starve.'

On other occasions, Dawson would challenge her beliefs.

'Can't you conceive of loving one man so much that you wouldn't want to compromise that love, before or after, by putting up with an imitation of it with someone else?'

'Do you really believe that stuff? One man?'

'I can assure you, it does come true for millions of people.'

'If one's never had any experience of other men, the one man might be the wrong one.'

'What is your conception of marriage, then?'

'Well, if you've got to have it at all, I suppose it's when you feel like settling down or having a baby or something and you like the boy you're with in particular, and so you just sort of go on . . . permanently. . .'

These discussions came to have less and less value as such to Dawson and Theresa. He did his best not so much to convince her as to keep her amused and entertained. She prepared herself less and less with arguments against religion, and more now with well-shaded eyes and pretty *jupes-culotte*.

One evening in January, Dawson had returned to the presbytery from an afternoon with Theresa and was sitting down to supper when another priest came in to say that there was an emergency call from Mrs Carter. Dawson went to the telephone: 'Please come,' she said. 'My husband has had an attack.'

Dawson picked up a small suitcase which contained the articles necessary for Extreme Unction, and went in a taxi to the house in Holland Park. Theresa opened the door. She was dressed in a long white dress, as if just going to a ball. Her face was tight with fear and bafflement. Dawson followed her upstairs. There, on the floor of the bedroom, lay the form of what he took to be Mr Carter. An ambulance orderly was holding an oxygen mask over his face: a doctor was punching the chest in the region of the heart. Mrs Carter, white-faced, sat on a chair. She stood up when Dawson entered but did not say a word.

Dawson went closer to the body. The orderly holding the mask took a metal clip in his free hand and forced it down between the tongue and the roof of the mouth. Then he re-applied the oxygen mask and inflated the body from the cylinder. As the gas came out of the lungs and stomach, the orderly tried to drag out Mr Carter's false teeth. 'Feel anything?' he asked the doctor. The doctor shook his head. 'Would you hold the mask, padre?' the doctor asked Dawson. Dawson knelt behind the head of grey hair and held the chipped metal and rubber mask over the mouth, the tongue between the teeth, slime bubbling where the oxygen still came through from the lungs.

The orderly whom he had replaced opened the doctor's case and took out an eight-inch needle. He fitted it to a syringe and filled the syringe with liquid from a small bottle. The doctor stopped kneading the body and took the syringe: he prodded the needle in the direction of the heart for a gap in the ribs. The body did not react. At the third thrust he found a gap, pushed the needle through and injected the liquid into the heart. The body still did not move. The eyes were half closed and bleary and showed no consciousness. The red face had no expression.

The orderly shook his head. The doctor rose and said: 'We'll take him to the hospital now, Mrs Carter.'

The woman's only reaction was to turn to the priest.

'Quick,' she said, 'quick, before they take him.'

'But was he . . .?' Dawson began to ask.

'Yes,' she said, 'yes, he was Catholic.'

Thus, while the doctor called the second orderly from the ambulance Dawson opened his small case and anointed the form of this man—either dead or nearly so. Then Mrs Carter went with her husband to the hospital. The doctor, the orderlies, the stretcher and the body—all were suddenly gone from the house. Dawson and Theresa went down to the drawing-room. She stood quivering by the unlit fire. Dawson may have felt, for a moment, superfluous: but then she looked at him with a great appeal in her eyes and her face creased up as she started to cry.

The priest took her awkwardly into his arms and comforted her.

'I wish you hadn't,' she said. Dawson did not answer because he did not hear. His mind still dwelt on the death he had just witnessed. He had anointed corpses before, but never had he seen life leave a body—the monstrous throttling of struggling lungs. Automatically he thought of God—but in place of the benign image there was a sour void. His mind turned back to death: if this ultimate horror was the end of life, then any happiness that preceded it was just a senseless fluttering around a flame, above all those joys of life's progression—love, marriage, birth.

'He never was a Catholic, I'm sure,' said Theresa. 'It was just Mum. . . . Oh God, how stupid.'

She sat down and he sat down next to her, attending at last to what she said. 'It made it easier for your mother,' he said automatically. 'And your father . . . he couldn't mind.'

'Yes, that's it, isn't it? Making it easier for her . . . that's all it is.' Theresa went on crying: then she stopped, stood up and went to a table where she poured two tumblers full of cognac. She came back to the sofa where they were sitting and gave one of them to Dawson. They both drank.

'Will you hold me again?' she asked.

'Of course,' he said, and again he took her in a comforting embrace.

'God, I loved him,' she said.

They remained like that for some time, sipping their brandy: but the comforting embrace did not comfort. It was unrelaxed for both of them, a touch of two bodies that did not calm and reassure but for different reasons tightened the minor ligaments and alarmed the nerves. And when the alcohol was in her blood and her thoughts were confused, the girl took the priest's head in her hands and kissed him on the lips. It was not a short kiss. She was quiet with concentration, putting her feelings and her experience into this gesture. He was still with horror and indecision, but eventually he stood and extracted himself and without words left the house. He prayed through the night to forgive and be forgiven but a grotesque image of her hair, her dress, her shoulders—the consistency of her flesh and the look in her eyes as he turned and left—this image would not leave him then or for many months afterwards.

Chapter Six

It was around this time that several London newspapers closed down. I was then a journalist on one whose future was precarious, and it was clear that if it was to survive, we must increase the circulation. One way in which it was thought that this might be done was to have a column of a religious nature and thereby attract some of the four million Catholics from their own papers—*The Universe* or *The Catholic Herald*. Not only would this increase in circulation be useful to us, but if it could be demonstrated that it included a proportion of prominent Catholics, it might draw advertising from the manufacturers of prefabricated confessionals, purveyors of altar wine and travel agents with cut-price pilgrimages to the Holy Land. There was a danger, of course, that sectarian articles would offend our regular readers: therefore it was decided that a radical, unorthodox priest would best suit our purpose. Dawson was well-known by this time for his sharp sermons on broad social questions. His name was mentioned. I spoke up, telling the editor of my acquaintance with this notorious priest and so was given the job of roping him in.

I recognized Dawson as he came through the doors of the Garrick Club, but only because he wore the black suit of a priest. The beaming young monk was now pale and his eyes avoided mine as we shook hands. But though I had not seen him for two years, I suddenly felt great affection for him and put my arm around his shoulder. He stood among the actors, publishers and other journalists, looking embarrassed and confused while I fetched the two drinks: we took them out of the bar into the library. We both agreed that we should have got together long ago. I started to tell him about some of the portraits on the wall, but he barely bothered to look at them.

'I hear that you're the Young Turk of Westminster these days,' I said.

'I don't think so . . . not really,' said Dawson, smiling.

'You don't look very well.'

'No. I'm rather tired.'

'It's harder work than at Kirkham, I dare say.'

'Yes.'

'But more worthwhile?'

'Yes . . . in a way.'

He turned to look at me for the first time. 'You see, a soul, a troubled soul, is just like a physical or a mental invalid. They need continuous attention—but of course there are thousands of them and very few of us.'

'A lot of what you do is sort of social work, isn't it?'

He frowned. 'It shouldn't be, really, but it's difficult to draw the line between the religious, the social and the psychiatric.'

We finished our drinks and went into the dining-room, where I had booked a table for a quarter past one. Dawson looked happier after his cocktail.

'I don't suppose you're a Catholic, these days, are you?' he asked me as we sat down.

'Not really,' I said.

'No, well, I didn't think you would be.'

'It all seemed irrelevant,' I said. 'I kept it up for a bit but then everyone else seemed to get on quite well without it so I gave it up.'

'Did any particular doctrine seem irrelevant?'

'Not really. I was quite prepared to believe in the Assumption of the Virgin and all that because it didn't affect me one way or the other: but chastity's absurd. That's the point of confrontation, I suppose.'

He picked up the menu and we both looked at it in silence.

I recommended the beef and he concurred. I also ordered some claret.

'Have you the same ambitions as you had at school?' I asked him.

'Good heavens, did I have ambitions?'

'Well, I don't know if they were ambitions, exactly. You wanted to help others. That sort of thing.'

'Oh yes. They were ambitions.'

'And you still have them?'

'Yes, but I'm a bit older. I can see that it's all rather more complicated than I thought.'

'Why?'

'Well, it's what I was saying before. There is plenty to do that would help others, but one doesn't always know what it is or how to do it—and then one makes mistakes.'

'Yes, but still you're a priest. You must have some answers to other people's problems.'

'Yes . . . as you say, I'm a priest.'

'Is that what you preach in your sermons?'

'Yes.'

'Isn't it preaching to the converted?'

It began to look as if Dawson was upset by this conversation. 'That's just it,' he said. 'So many of those who need one's help aren't even Catholics: in fact they're against Catholicism.'

'You should preach to the unconverted.'

'At Hyde Park Corner?'

'No. Through newspapers.'

'Do you mean *The Catholic Herald* or something like that?'

'No. That again would be to the converted.'

Our lunch was set down before us. We stopped our conversation while this was done.

'We want to put a column of a religious nature in our paper,' I said.

'Do you think the irreligious would read it?'

'Well, they might if the articles were lively and more on morals than theology, if you see what I mean.'

'And controversial?'

'Yes.'

'It might work.'

'Would you write them?'

He looked me in the eyes again. 'I don't know that I'd be competent.'

'Why not?'

'Well, I've never written anything.'

'If you can write a sermon, you can write an article.'

'Perhaps.'

'It would be an opportunity.'

'Yes.'

'A lot of people are interested in religion who never go into a church.'

'I know.'

'Many of them need some sort of solace and guidance.'

'Yes.'

'It'd be once a month or once a fortnight. Quite short. Four or five hundred words. You might save a thousand souls.'

'One would be enough.'

'Exactly.'

'If you're no longer Catholic . . .?'

'Business,' I said, and smiled.

'All right,' he said, 'I'll have to ask permission.'

'Will you get it?'

'Oh yes.'

Three weeks later Dawson sent in his first article and it seemed to be just what we wanted. It attacked the concept of separate religious education and provoked several hundred letters over the next few days. The second and third articles turned on the missions and the nursing orders. His 'errors', from the orthodox point of view, were in the line of Jansenism—doubt of the religious significance of good works. I think he had two types in mind: first the man who believes in God but finds little way in which he can apply his faith, either because his environment or his own weakness prevent him from earning God's approbation. Secondly, he was thinking of the atheistic humanitarian—the man who dedicates himself to mankind without any expectation of reward in an after-life.

Dawson said that belief was enough. Do not confuse faith with humanitarianism. Sympathy for your fellow man is not a religious sentiment but an animal emotion. Like other forms of human love—sensual, parental or brotherly love—it is of no theological significance. Thus Christians are not notably more humanitarian than non-Christians. We help others in obedience to an instinct that preserves the unity of society: Faith in God is quite another question.

I hope I have paraphrased his position correctly. It was never stated so specifically, but was implied in what he said on concrete issues. In his fourth article he said that a man could not and should not be expected to obey rules which he felt, in his conscience, caused unhappiness in others. His example, of course, was the Church's ruling on contraception, but he went on to say, in conjectural terms, that the time might come when pre-marital sexual intercourse would be acceptable to a large number of Christian individuals. This caused trouble. We printed protesting letters from orthodox priests, and in answer to them Dawson made his strongest protest yet: why does the Church concern itself so much with life that is only theoretical (as in the contraceptive issue) when it is so callous about real life—in Nazi Germany or Vietnam?

Until this time hard work had kept his mind from introspection: but now, late at night, when he wrote his articles, he started to examine and question his behaviour in relation to his beliefs. All the while he continued to practise his priestly office with the professionalism of a doctor or a lawyer, never again becoming involved with an individual. He baptized babies and anointed corpses, heard sins and forgave them. He talked to engaged couples, arranged their dispensations, signed their certificates and married them. There were children to be taught truths and others to be persuaded that these were indeed truths, that God had made them to know, love and serve him, that there was a heaven where they might be happy, a place where the tediousness and compromise of their lives would be transmuted into a luxuriant well-being of an ill-defined sort, etc.

But what evidence was there that people were any better off for all this? He had lived long enough now to know that happiness was an elusive quality in our lives but it was possible to identify suffering, and the absence of suffering was as good a definition of happiness as any. Since his life was dedicated to helping others, he had only to ask himself if he assisted in alleviating their suffering. The answer he came up with was that he did not. The State had taken care of Helen Sweet. With Theresa he had caused suffering: he perhaps caused it when he refused absolution to women in over-crowded flats who took measures to prevent themselves having children. He even felt he caused suffering in parting illicit lovers or teaching children to examine their consciences and invent guilt they did not feel.

His sixth article never reached us. It was to have been something about there being no sin against God but only against our fellow men, but he rang me one afternoon to say that he had been asked by his superiors not to deliver it. It had been suggested, he said, that he go into retreat at a monastery of Trappist monks in Cumberland. He explained that they were not the same as the monks at Kirkham. They did not teach but worked a farm and kept complete silence. He said that it was customary for the secular clergy from Westminster to go there for periods of spiritual recuperation.

He was apologetic and sounded confused: I was sorry for him and said that there would be no trouble over the contract, though I knew we would have difficulty in finding someone else.

Cumberland has a bare and gloomy landscape—stark hills crossed with stone walls. The stone is hard and the buildings that men have made with it are stocky and inelegant, built to resist cold rain and wind. The Trappist monastery at Pixhaven comprised a few neo-Gothic buildings, all overlooking a lake, five fir trees, a church, a farm, a barn and seventeen monks. One of the buildings was a guest house, and Dawson was given a room there with a view back on to a hill-side of grey shale.

He did not know what he was expected to do. The monks seemed to have a routine quite different to that at Kirkham: they rose at two in the morning. Dawson was wakened by this bell on the first night, but he decided that he was there for a rest and so went back to sleep again. He rose at seven and went to say mass but could find no one to serve him. He asked the porter at the door if there was anyone available: this brother made signs to signify that he understood the problem and that he himself would serve Father Dawson.

The prior, of course, was permitted to speak and at eleven Dawson was asked, through gestures, to visit him. He was a small, dark man and not much older than Dawson himself.

'You were at Kirkham once, weren't you?' asked the prior.

'Yes. I was transferred . . . not long ago.'

'Do you prefer the secular clergy?'

'I think I'm more suited to it.'

'I don't know how long you're expected to stay here, do you?'

'Not really. The archbishop . . .'

'I know. Yes. He thought you needed a rest.'

'Yes.'

'I wonder if this is the sort of rest . . . I mean to say, the South of France might have been a better idea.'

Dawson laughed. 'I don't think so,' he said.

'Well, I'll tell you what it's like here and you can join in just as you like. We begin at two in the morning and end at nine in the evening. It's just Saint Benedict's rule without what they call the reforms. It'll be interesting for you to compare us with Kirkham. We spend about six hours a day singing the *Opus Dei*; then another five or six at manual labour which here is mainly milking the cows and seeing to the sheep. Then the rest of the day is spent in prayer, meditation and study. Silence is strictly observed, except for directions at work and consultations with superiors and that sort of thing. You can come to me any time you like, if you feel you have something to discuss. We eat at twelve and five and I'll see you get some proper food. We only eat vegetables, you see, but there's no reason why you shouldn't have some meat and eggs.'

Dawson was astonished that this prior was so unlike any of the monks at Kirkham—even Father Maximilian whom he had always seen as the nearest they had to a Trappist. The prior was more like a business man, with the same thick spectacles and quick manner of talking. He told Dawson that he had trained to be a barrister.

Dawson thanked him and left and went down to the church to say his office. After he had done this, after he had mouthed the prescribed paragraphs from his breviary, he sat wondering what he should do. He thought he should say some more prayers, personal prayers, words of his own spoken to God as an individual, not as a priest. But he found that he had nothing to say, nothing that was not a repetition of the sorrow, glory and thanks he had said already. There was nothing he wanted to pray for, nothing that needed his prayers.

He went out of the church and started to walk away from the monastery up the hill. The grass was short and close, enclosing the rocks like a liquid that had hardened. It was cold but not wet. He turned and looked down on the few buildings. He could see some of the monks carrying pails from one out-house to another. He tried to pray. Someone was always in need of prayer. He considered praying for the conversion of non-Catholics but the idea provoked an almost physical repugnance. Such prayers seemed like inept intrusion into the privacy of others. He wanted to think of ways in which Catholicism benefited man, but the revulsion again spread from his mind to his body. He reacted for a moment to the thought of God as to the beginning of a tedious story that he had heard many times before. One cannot bear to listen, but cannot turn away or block one's ears: there is nothing to do but await the inescapable boredom.

He started to walk further up the mountain and reached the shale. He then walked across it, the stone and shingle sliding away under his feet. He kept his balance and reached the other side: and then turned to look at the spot where, if he had fallen, he might have broken his neck. He had not noticed the height, for he was distracted by a terrifying inner vertigo.

Dawson climbed back down the hill and reached the monastery again. He sat in his room, opened a book, shut it again. Though he did not particularly want to, he went to the lavatory and urinated. He washed his hands and went back to his room where he lay on the bed and might have gone to sleep if the midday bell had not rung.

He stood and automatically started to say the Angelus. But after he had said 'the angel of the Lord declared unto Mary' he could not go on. He waited for the interval of time that it would have taken him to finish the prayer, and then left the guest house for the refectory. There thirteen monks sat at one long table. Two other monks served their brothers. Dawson sat down at one end and was served with first a plate of vegetables and two pork sausages. The monks were served with the same vegetables, but on their plates were no sausages.

There was brown bread and there was water. No one spoke. Eventually one of the serving monks read from some work of Cardinal Newman.

All kept their eyes lowered and their glances straight but Dawson became aware of the presence of his two pork sausages as he had never been aware of pork sausages before. The sound as he sliced them seemed to be heard all around him, and the chewing of this animal's flesh seemed so that it must reek to all the rest of them. The nerves tightened in his stomach: he was barely able to finish.

After lunch Dawson went up to the prior's room again. It was empty but he waited there. The desk was piled with books, all of a religious sort. He looked away from them out of the window: from here too there was a view of the sombre side of the hill. How hard it had been, he thought, to eat those sausages: yet how easy to swallow the beef with his irreligious friend in the Garrick Club.

The prior came in behind him.

'Are you finding anything to do?' he asked Dawson.

'No. I'm afraid I can't really stand it.'

'Yes, well, when I saw you, I thought it was a mistake.'

'I'm sorry I seem so ungrateful.'

'Not at all. Does it remind you of Kirkham?'

'No. It's not that. I'm afraid I can't seem to pray here.'

'Yes.'

'What do you pray about?'

'About? Well, it's not really a question of praying about anything . . .'

'I mean, do you pray for the conversion of Russia and that sort of thing?'

'No.'

'Do you think other people benefit from your prayers?'

'Yes.' The prior leant against his desk.

'Aren't you tampering with their free will?'

'I don't think it's quite as direct as that.'

'Then what's the use?'

'It's more a question of acting on their behalf. Outside, after all, one is distracted by anxieties of one kind or another.'

'And not inside?'

'Of a sort, perhaps. But there's no necessity for that element of animal nature that a man needs in the world.'

'Is that why you don't eat meat?'

'Well . . . something like that.'

'It seems to me . . . I don't know . . . that you attach evil to something innocent like an egg or a sausage.'

The prior said nothing.

'In what way . . . ,' said Dawson, 'can you think of any way in which a Catholic is better or better off than a non-Catholic?'

'Of course. If nothing else, he can receive the body of Christ in Holy Communion.'

'Yes, I know . . . but that doesn't make them any less malicious, impatient and unkind than anyone else, does it?'

'No. Perhaps not.'

'I don't know,' said Dawson more quietly, 'I don't mean to attack you or the Church. One becomes so confused with the bishops blessing guns and one's own mistakes.'

'You should read what Christ himself said.'

'Yes, I know, but I'm tired of those two columns of black type.'

'You really should have gone to Nice,' said the prior. 'I'm afraid you're just tired of the clerical life.'

'And bored with God.'

'That shouldn't be possible.'

'One only loses Faith through one's own fault, isn't that true?'

'Yes.'

'One's own, conscious fault?'

'Yes.'

'I'm very much afraid that that is what I have done.'

When I saw Dawson again in London I was astonished by the difference in his appearance. Physically he was the same—a tall, lean figure with only his hair grown slightly longer. The change was in his mood and never have I seen a man so affected by it. We met in the same Club but this time he beamed at me as we came up the steps.

'Your holiday seems to have done you good,' I said.

'It has,' he said, 'though not in the way they expected.'

We had our drinks—remaining in the bar this time: his ebullience was so marked that his voice quite easily rose above the noise made by the other members.

'What happened?' I asked.

'I'm getting out,' he said.

'What?'

'I'm giving up the priesthood.'

I was confounded and could not think of anything to say, but that did not seem to matter to him. 'To my future,' he said, raising his glass of gin-and-tonic. 'I'm a late starter so I'll need some luck.'

'Yes,' I said and raised my glass. But somehow the idea of Dawson out of his clerical clothes upset me.

'Why?' I asked him.

'I didn't think you'd need to ask me. . . . Because I don't believe in it any more, in any of it. Not even in God. I've reached my maturity at long last. I've outgrown all the nonsense that we were taught at Kirkham and now I want to live as deeply as I can before I die.'

'Then you've abandoned your ambition?'

'Not at all. I shall be more likely to realize it. I haven't been of much use to anyone as a priest, but now as a man I might be able to do something.'

'In what way?'

'Well, I hoped you might be able to advise me. I thought I might make a journalist.'

'Yes . . . you already are one.'

'Have you any idea of how I might set about it?'

Dawson looked so excited by the idea that I hated to discourage him, though at that moment I felt his chances would be small. I knew that my colleagues were mostly narrow-minded and jealous and unlikely to admit a newcomer if they could avoid doing so.

'It depends on the kind of journalist you want to be,' I said.

'I don't know. I'd take anything, really.'

It occurred to me that Dawson was not just my school friend but a de-frocked priest and that that, journalistically, was a valuable title to hold . . . but then I put the idea out of my mind, assuming that he would not want to prostitute his past in any way.

'What was it like, after so long, losing faith?' I asked.

'Horrible at first. After all, one's questioning one's identity in a way. Who am I, if not a priest? I went through days when I thought I was mad and might kill myself because everything was so unsure. It was like waking up on top of St Paul's Cathedral: one's first reaction is not to admire the view but to feel quite terrified. It was a kind of vertigo—fear and giddiness. But then I gradually came down and began to enjoy simple things like the taste of food and the smell of air . . . things I'd never really noticed before. And now . . . now I'm not only happy, but I've recovered all those ambitions to be of some use to the world.'

I thought him naïve, of course, but he did look happy. He said he hoped to be released from his vows without much difficulty since he had a history of vocational instability. We agreed that we would meet again when all this had gone through, and that meanwhile I would keep my eyes open for him.

Chapter Seven

The day of departure. The prospect of an end to the sad, angry, baffled glances of the other priests. There were sudden problems of a practical sort. What clothes should he wear? Besides his priest's clothes, he had only the grey flannel trousers and white shirt he had worn to the youth club. He put these on in the morning and went to a shop opposite Victoria Station. He bought a brown sports coat, a white shirt, a yellow tie, brown socks and at another shop brown shoes.

He was afraid that the shop assistant would guess why he wanted the clothes—a complete outfit like that—but there was no expression of surprise and no questions. It was, after all, an area of London where no human behaviour would seem strange. Dawson returned to the presbytery, his clothes in three different packages. There was, then, nothing left to do but change into them and depart. He did this, and left his priest's clothes neatly folded on a chair in his room, for though he owned them (a secular priest does not take the vow of poverty), they could be of no further use to him. He had taken his official leave the day before and had been given three hundred pounds in ten pound notes as back pay which he had paid into an account in a bank. There was no one else he had any reason to see. He therefore packed his personal belongings—pyjamas, razor, underclothes, grey flannels, white shirt, socks and black shoes—into a small canvas bag and left the room. He closed its door. He walked down the corridor which smelt of polish and down the stairs. No one was around, not even the porter. He hesitated for a moment in the dark hall by the visiting rooms: then he went out into the street, closing the door of the presbytery behind him.

He had plans, first to visit his mother, then his sister. He had three hours before the train left for York from King's Cross station: and in that time he wanted to equip himself more fully with the appurtenances of the layman. He walked down Victoria Street, then turned off at Broadway and crossed St James's Park. He walked up Lower Regent Street to Piccadilly and there went into a department store. He had no list of what he needed, but hoped that he would be reminded by what was on display. He went first to the basement and bought a suitcase; then to the second floor where he picked out a dark grey suit, tried it on and bought it for cash. He went down again to the ground floor and bought two more shirts—one checked and one striped: then a dressing-gown and some bedroom slippers. He put them all into the suitcase as he bought them. He explained to each salesman that all his luggage had been stolen at the airport. They seemed to believe him.

Near the entrance to the shop there were counters for socks and ties, tobacco and shaving accessories. Dawson bought some coloured socks, but hesitated over the ties—a guinea each. Suddenly he smelt a strong scent: he glanced towards the *toiletteries* as if to see if that was its source, but as his face turned to the left, another face, a woman's, came round to meet his from the right. He turned back again and found himself staring into this woman's eyes.

'I thought it was you,' she said.

Dawson smiled. He could not remember who she was.

'What are you doing here?' she asked. 'I don't suppose you'll find many lost souls in Simpsons.' She gave an ironical twist to her mouth.

She looked at his tie, his sports coat, his suitcase. 'You are Father Dawson, aren't you?'

'Yes,' he said.

'Thank goodness. It would have been very embarrassing if you weren't. You are rather . . . well . . . in disguise, aren't you?' She smiled, looking straight into his eyes.

'Yes, I'm afraid I am.'

'Well, I won't keep you. I just wanted to say hallo and tell you that my troubles are all over now.'

'Good. I'm glad.'

'I wish you'd come and see us,' she said. 'I'll tell you all about it.'

'Yes,' said Dawson.

'My number's in the book.' The woman smiled and walked on out of the shop.

Dawson returned to the ties and bought two of them. He still smelt the scent. He went over to the counter of soaps and bought, haphazardly, deodorant, talcum powder, eau-de-cologne and after-shave lotion. He next crossed to the smoking counter and bought a briar pipe and a tin of Sobranie tobacco. Then he remembered that the woman was Jenny Stanten—someone he had baptized and instructed a year before. What had she meant by saying that her troubles were over? He had a vague recollection that she had been unhappily married; perhaps now the husband and wife were reconciled.

In the train he tried the pipe. At first he felt that there might be some enjoyment in sucking the smoke into his mouth and in forming an atmosphere of his own around his head: but as the nicotine and tar collected in the stem, the pipe itself began to taste bitter. Dawson finished it and became revolted by the filthy object in his hands. He stood up and went out into the corridor. There, surreptitiously so that the other passengers would not see, he threw the pipe out of an open window.

He returned to his compartment and read the newspaper he had bought at the station. Then he studied the faces of the other passengers. They all seemed ordinary enough, and the women plain, but they were not uncomfortable in his presence. A yellow tie and a brown jacket were less arresting than a black suit and a clerical collar.

He thought of Jenny Stanten, of meeting her like that in the middle of a city of ten million, of how lovely she was and how well dressed, and of the slimness of the calves of her legs that he had glimpsed as she had gone up the steps of the shop into the street.

His mother was at the station to meet him and she drove him home in her car. Of course they kissed each other at the barrier, but Dawson could sense at once that she was not interested in him—in his loss of faith or his future. She started at once to tell him of her own preoccupations—he was among them—as if to scotch an account of his grander turbulence of fate.

'It's your life, Eddie, and you must do with it as you like. It's quite natural that you should want a change. Mrs Harrison's son worked with Yorkshire Insurance until he was thirty-one and then decided all at once, just like that, that he wanted to be a doctor and that's just what he's doing. It's a little strange, because it takes five or six years, doesn't it? But I suppose he hasn't got any family to pay for and he can go on living at home. What do you think you'll do, Eddie? The ladies at the office do sometimes ask about you, you know. You won't remember any of them, but they remember you. . . .

'Now someone like your father would have worried awfully because we all lived through the depression years, you know, and even people with a good education sometimes had a terrible time finding work. But nowadays there seems to be plenty of it. At least there is in York. They say that up in Newcastle it isn't so good. It's all right in London, I should think. Are you going back there? Sally's in Leeds, you know. I told you that she married that Arnold didn't I? She didn't ask you to the wedding, did she? Well there wasn't much of one. I didn't mind about it not being in a church, because she doesn't believe in it and neither does Arnold . . . isn't it an awful name, Arnold? There wasn't even a reception, not even a party. Just the business in the registry office. Evidently Arnold doesn't believe in weddings or something. Of course they'd been living together for some time before so I suppose it wasn't very, well, very different afterwards. They only told me the day before. Perhaps you'll get married now, will you? The Dean's daughter is awfully nice. She worked with us for six months, but I think she's going to do something in Africa now. . . .'

Three days later, Dawson went to Leeds to see his sister. Her husband was a research chemist at the university. They had, by now, a child. She too met him at the station: she looked detached, but was not unfriendly to him.

'You've never seen Jamie, have you?' she asked.

'Never. Nor your husband.'

'No . . . well, it makes things easier, your not being a priest any more. Arnie hates religion.'

'You've given it all up?'

'Never had it, really.'

'It took me a long time.'

'Yes, well, that awful school. Poor Mum. How was she?'

'She doesn't seem to mind much about anything.'

'No. I don't suppose she does. She's happy inside her own little world. Did you meet her collection of old witches at the Charity?'

'No, I didn't. Do you go across there much?'

'Oh yes . . . at week-ends. On the way to Scarborough. And she comes over here sometimes when she wants to do some shopping. But there's only the couch. I hope you won't mind.'

Their home was the third floor of a fifty-year-old house which had been converted into flats. Arnold, Sally's husband, was sitting in an armchair with an empty pipe in his mouth.

He looked around when Dawson came in and stood up a few minutes later.

'This is Eddie,' Sally said to him.

'Nice to meet you,' Arnold said. 'I hardly knew Sal had a brother until she told me you were coming.'

Arnold never looked directly at Dawson, nor at Sally, nor at his son, Jamie, as if so much demand was made of his eyes at the laboratory that they would not be spared for expression at home. He wore imitation horn-rimmed spectacles and had hair brushed forward into a fringe to hide the areas where he was going bald.

'Are you thinking of moving up here?' he asked Dawson as Sally went into the kitchen to make tea.

'I haven't really thought. I think I'll probably stay in London, since I know it.'

'You'll find more chances up here, you know.'

'I dare say: but I do have a few contacts down there.'

'Contacts. Yes. You need contacts in London. No one's judged on their merits alone down there, are they? It all goes on who you know. There are a few chaps you were at school with, I suppose?' ('Chaps' spoken with affectation.)

'Yes, well, one or two . . . and others.'

'Of course most people who live in London think it's the bloody end of the world up here, but I can tell you that there's more that gets done up here than down there. And it's real work. You won't find any of your glamour industries in Leeds.'

'I haven't really thought of what I'm going to do.'

'Not qualified for much, are you?'

'No.'

'With that posh voice of yours, you won't find it difficult.'

'I have a friend who's in journalism.'

'Well, you're all set up, aren't you?'

'Yes, if I want to go into journalism, I think he'd find me something.'

'Journalism's all right if you've nothing better to do,' said Arnie.

After tea Arnold said he had work to do at the laboratory. Dawson read the *Yorkshire Evening Press* while Sally put her whining child to bed. Eventually she joined her brother in the living-room.

'Well,' she asked, 'what would you like to do?'

'What do you usually do?'

She smiled and nodded at the television set in front of them. 'Do you smoke or anything?' she asked, taking a cigarette and handing the pack to him. Her hands were scrubbed and red: her face was thinner, accentuating its sharp features. She had cut her hair short, which more than anything else had changed her appearance.

'I don't smoke,' said Dawson. 'Let's watch television.' Sally leant over and turned it on. They both stared at it—the regional news—and then she asked: 'Well, what are you going to do, with your life, I mean?'

'I thought you might have had some ideas.'

'I don't know. I mean you couldn't do much that needs a long training, could you, like a doctor or an architect or anything like that?'

'Not really.'

'Have you any cash at all?'

'About two hundred and fifty pounds.'

'Well, that's not bad. At least you can look around for a few weeks . . . but be careful of rent. We spent the first year in a flat, renting it, and it just wasn't worth it. I mean you're just there to watch telly and eat and sleep, aren't you? We got this place on a mortgage.'

'Is that cheaper?'

'Not cheaper, no. But at least you've got something to show for it. It's not much of a place. We could get another because I'm working again now, but Arnie's not sure if he's staying here or not.'

'Might you move?'

'He tried for a job in Birmingham but he didn't get it. There aren't many openings in his line of research. He's had an offer from a big American company in Minnesota, if you know where that is. I don't. Somewhere in the middle. They'd pay a lot but . . . I don't know . . . they say that prices are much higher and Mum'd be left on her own: and there's no knowing that we'd like it any better over there. . . .'

Sally smiled at him. Dawson felt a real affection for her. Their coming together again was surely the first benefit of his leaving the priesthood.

'Is Arnies' work important?' he asked Sally. 'Is he on to something, or what?'

'Don't ask me,' she said. 'I don't really understand it and he never explains, you know. Very few scientific discoveries are dramatic, though, like penicillin. Arnie's field is synthetics, which is why he came to the university up here. He thought he might interest some of the cloth people with his ideas: but they're very conservative. The Americans are the only ones likely to find a commercial application.'

'But he lives for his work, does he?'

Sally looked down at her skirt and said: 'You must stop thinking of people as living for something. Most people live because that's the way they find themselves.'

The television programme had changed but neither watched nor listened.

'But you are happy, aren't you?' Dawson asked his sister.

'Oh yes,' she said, standing. 'We've had some good times. You'd like some tea, wouldn't you?'

Dawson studied his sister, her husband, her son, for the three days that he was there. They seemed always distracted from talking to each other and to him by the newspapers in the morning, television in the evening and, to judge by the paperbacks on their bedside table, by reading at night. When they went for a walk, they were distracted by the child: clothing him, carrying him, preventing him from running into puddles. The child was left at a nursery during the day when they worked, though Sally came back at three. She then withdrew into caring for Jamie, and Arnie withdrew into his work or into the political events of the day, which provoked disparaging remarks made with no expectation of a reply. The conversation between husband and wife was practical: let's take Jamie for a walk before it rains: peas or carrots; there's a Humphrey Bogart on Channel Two.

Dawson did not get on with his brother-in-law. Arnie thought, and said, that anyone who had ever been a Catholic priest, defrocked or not, was sort of soft-brained: and Dawson . . . well, instinctively, he still checked the more uncharitable of his trains of thought.

From a room in the Great Northern Hotel in London, Dawson started to look for a flat. Most of them were not only expensive, but required a deposit—'key money'—or a lease. He had thought of paying five pounds a week, but soon realized that he would be lucky to find one for ten. After five days he found a place with two dark rooms besides a kitchen and bathroom. It was two miles up the Edgware road and cost nine pounds a week. The furniture was worn and stained by the many different people who had lived there before him. Dawson bought some sheets and a pillow-case of his own: a cup and saucer, a plate, two knives, a fork, a small pot and a frying-pan. He went out a second time to get a tea-pot, a spoon, some tea, milk, bread, butter, eggs, marmalade, salt, pepper, a frozen chicken and a tin of peas. That evening he cooked himself supper—the chicken fried in butter, the peas heated in the pan, bread butter and tea.

Next day, after breakfast, he went out to a public call-box and rang me at the paper. We made an appointment for lunch in two days' time. He then took a bus down to Marble Arch and went for a walk in Hyde Park. He watched the other people who were there—many of them alone like himself. At one he went to a cafeteria and had a bowl of soup, and cod and chips. Then he fetched a cup of coffee and sat drinking it. Across the room, filled with secretaries and Oxford Street shoppers, young trainees and messenger boys, he saw another man eating alone, slowly and deliberately, but this man was badly dressed—almost a tramp—while Dawson knew that he was well-dressed in his grey suit and striped shirt.

In the afternoon he went to a film—an aesthetic treatment of an adulterous love affair. He came out of the cinema at five, bought two pork chops, some frozen carrots and a bag of potatoes. He took these back to his flat and cooked them. When he had finished his supper, he left the flat and went to the nearest pub and ordered a pint of beer. There were several other people there but Dawson was shy and did not appear open to conversation with a stranger. He drank the beer and went back to the flat. He started to read a novel, *Anna Karenina*, but found he was drowsy, so he went to bed.

I believe that I was the first person he can have talked to for any length of time since he had left his sister in Leeds. We met again at the Garrick Club: Dawson wore his grey suit and check shirt. He looked so ill-at-ease in these clothes that I immediately felt sorry for not having seen him before. I could have taken him to my tailor and advised him on shirts and ties.

'How are you getting on?' I asked.

'I must say, it's not easy,' he said. 'I feel as if I was fifteen or sixteen years old.'

'Yes, a lot of . . . well . . . ex-priests evidently have a hard time. There's some kind of organization . . .'

Dawson lifted his hand. 'I know,' he said.

'No,' I said quickly. 'I didn't mean for you. You won't need anything like that. Once you've got something to do and know a few more people, it'll all be easy enough. You'll probably regret those days of peace and quiet. I find I don't have the time to think of what I'm doing. I get carried in and out with the tide.'

Dawson chose the roast beef again: I myself had a salmon salad.

'I hope you still want to come into journalism,' I said.

'Do you think I'd be able to do it?'

'It's quite clearly your vocation,' I said.

Dawson smiled.

'And I've a proposition,' I went on.

'You mustn't feel responsible for me,' he said. 'I just wanted some advice, really.'

'On the contrary. I expect you to be one of my most valuable assets—but wait and see what I've got to say because it isn't much and you may turn it down flat. It's an assistant editorship on a suburban newspaper, the *Gazette* in Beaconsfield. There's an old editor there at the moment but he wants to move on. You could spend a month or two learning about it and then take over.'

'That's very good of you,' said Dawson. 'Are you sure they'd take me on?'

'Yes, of course, I said. It belongs to a friend of mine.'

'I see.'

'I still see you as a feature writer,' I said, 'doing the kind of thing you did before for us: but perhaps some experience of the administration of a paper like the *Gazette* would equip you better in an all-round way.'

The truth was that at that time I could not see any possibilities in feature writing that would make him a living. He undoubtedly had a talent for the kind of crusading article he had written before, but I imagined that their interest to the public came from his being a priest. In a short time I was to be proved quite wrong, but in somewhat special circumstances.

Dawson seemed worried by the thought of leaving London, having just found himself a flat: but I told him that he could easily commute to Beaconsfield. The paper was a weekly: it came out on Thursdays and he needed only to go down on the two days before it went to press.

After lunch we walked through Leicester Square to Piccadilly. His salary was to be eighteen hundred a year, which he seemed to think lavish, but I knew he had no real concept of the cost of living. He asked me where I bought my clothes and I told him, though I warned him off some of the more expensive places. We walked up Bond Street together. I had an appointment at three so we parted on the corner of Hanover Square.

As I have said, thirty-five pounds a week seemed to Dawson at the time to be a great deal of money: but tax and social security took eight of them, the rent and rates took ten or eleven more and the train fares to Beaconsfield, three on top of that. He did manage to live on it, however, buying some more clothes, a small gramophone and a ticket to the theatre every now and then.

His great problem, of course, was the lack of acquaintances on whom he could now call. All those he had known before had been Catholic and there is no loathing like that of a Catholic for a priest who has gone back on his vows. The people on the *Gazette* all lived in Beaconsfield: the editor did ask him home one evening, but Dawson found him dull and had to leave early to catch the last train back to London. Perhaps he expected more from me, though he told me later that he always thought that our friendship was something of an aberration in both of us.

For a time, then, he was as lonely as a layman as he had been as a priest: but he felt this loneliness more acutely because of the question of women. What protective inhibitions there had been in his mind when he had lived under the vow of chastity had now entirely left him and he reacted as any other man of his age to the tableaux of titillation and innuendo that he saw all around him in London. The advertisements for films, brassieres or beer showed pretty girls with their legs apart, their bosoms round like ostrich eggs. Novels, even Tolstoy, and music, even Mozart, seemed to exalt the joy of love and its physical expression. He felt the urgency of finding a mate, but how was he to do it? Friendless, inexperienced, how could he even enter the atmosphere around a woman in which flirtation could begin? When he took his clothes to the launderette, he saw girls, both young and pretty, but many of them were clearly married or attached. How was he to tell between those who were already in love and those who were available? He imagined that to make a mistake in such a situation would be so gross that even a yearning as acute as his could not justify the risk. He was not desperate just for the physical sensation of intercourse, for which he might have paid a prostitute, but for love, for loving words and affectionate gestures. He was not ambitious for a beautiful or intelligent woman: any decent girl would have contented him. But he was a hunter without licence or gun or any knowledge of traps and snares—and his only prospect was to catch a glimpse of his game scuttling around him.

I once asked him, rather insensitively, why he had not called the Carters. At that time, when the irony of this omission was very clear, he simply shrugged and said he did not know. I imagine that he thought he had so grossly wounded and offended Theresa Carter two years before that no friendship could be salvaged from the debris. Or perhaps he was ashamed to face the mother. In any case, the love he had in mind was something gentle and calm: not a tortured confrontation of extreme and painful emotion.

Eight

One morning in June, while dabbing his freshly shaven face with sweet, astringent lotion, Dawson was reminded of Jenny Stanten: and he decided that he would call her as she had invited him to do. Her number was in the directory, but he hesitated for two days before daring to telephone. He felt that she might have forgotten who he was, that she might be offended by his having left the Church, or that her husband might misinterpret his motives in asking to visit them. On the other hand, she might be able to introduce him to a circle of people and among them might be an available girl.

In the end, he took hold of himself and dialled the number given in the directory. It was eleven in the morning. A child's voice answered.

'May I speak to Mrs Stanten?' he asked.

'Who is it?' the child asked.

'Edward Dawson.'

There were sounds of movement from the telephone: a child climbing down from a chest or a chair, and then a shout for its mother and the giving of his name.

'Well, hello,' said the voice of Jenny Stanten.

'You said I might call.'

'I did indeed. When can you come and see us?'

'Any time.'

'Can you make it this evening?'

'Certainly. That would be very nice.'

'What about her husband?' Dawson asked himself, as he stood at the door of the Stantens' eighteenth-century house in Chelsea. The door was then opened by a tiny girl of five or six dressed in her night-gown. She did not say a word but toddled back into the house, proud to have turned the handle. Dawson followed and found himself in a room panelled in dark wood. This room acted as a hall. There were old macintoshes and Wellington boots up against the wall. He followed the little girl upstairs: she said nothing but concentrated on the climb and he on keeping step behind her. She led him into a large room which seemed to cover the whole of the first floor: its walls were white; there were bookcases, a Chinese screen, Rothkos, Persian rugs, a deep sofa, armchairs and small tables—everything beautiful in itself and in elegant disorder.

Jenny Stanten came in behind him—the mistress of this London house with its long windows. She was then only twenty-six or so, and was what one might call a fashionable beauty. Her features were gentle, uniform and calm. The blue of her eyes matched the blue of her long skirt: her skin was as pale as the cotton of her blouse. Her straight blonde hair framed an excellent work in the medium of shadow and mascara: and more powerful than her scent, Pinget's 'Fracas', was her slim, nonchalant body and the warm, direct look that came from her eyes—glances which appealed and smiled and looked suddenly melancholy, all within the span of a minute.

Dawson had forgotten how lovely and graceful she was: when he had instructed her he had not noticed that kind of thing. He began to admire her now, from the moment she came into the room, but the moment of conscious enjoyment was short and was soon overtaken by so complete a feeling of pleasure in her presence that there was no margin in his feelings for detached appreciation. It was . . . well, schoolgirls have a phrase for it—love at first sight.

'How nice of you to call,' she said. 'I'd rather given up hope.'

'I didn't know if I should or not,' said Dawson, 'now that I'm no longer . . .'

'Yes,' she said, 'I know all about that. What should I call

you now? Mister Dawson?' (Smile.)

'Edward. It was my . . . original name.'

'Edward. Fine. I hope I don't slip up and call you Father Dawson.'

'Don't worry.'

'Was it awful?' she asked, pouring whisky on to ice in a large, polished glass.

'What?'

'Losing faith . . . leaving?'

'No,' he said, 'not so bad. It's like growing up at last.'

'At last,' she repeated. 'I can imagine.'

'But one doesn't regard one's childhood as a waste of time, however long it lasts.' Dawson took up the drink she had poured for him.

They both sat down on the deep, wide sofa. Jenny leaned back in one corner. Dawson crouched on the edge.

'It was the time afterwards that was difficult,' he said to this attentive, sympathetic girl beside him. 'I was lonely as a priest . . . most priests are lonely—but now I've lost what friends I had.'

'People are so intolerant,' she said.

'No. It's only natural. A priest means a lot to them: they lean their uncertainties on him, and so, if he falls, they find it hard to keep standing.'

Dawson looked into his drink, drank some of it, then looked back at Jenny. 'And you?' he asked. 'You said that your troubles were over.'

'Yes,' she said quietly looking straight into his face. 'My husband died.'

'I'm sorry,' Dawson said.

'Don't be sorry. I wasn't.'

Dawson said nothing.

'It was a car crash,' she said, guessing at what he would not allow himself to think. 'I was with him.'

'Were you injured?'

'Not badly. I am, as you see, intact.' She smiled again.

'That was lucky.'

'Providential. I haven't said a prayer since because I don't know who did me the favour—Pan or Zeus or Neptune or Wotan or Christ or Mohammed. . . .' She laughed.

Dawson sat back in the sofa and rested his head on a cushion. The alcohol seeping into his blood, he moved his eyes to the right and looked at Jenny—her long legs under the cotton of her skirt, her hair swept back behind her ear on the side of her head that faced him.

'Or perhaps you put in a word for me?' she asked.

'It was my last prayer,' he said and they both laughed. Jenny stood up and fetched the bottle of whisky. She poured more of it into their glasses.

'That was nearly a year ago,' she said. 'Your dramatic event was more recent, wasn't it?'

'That morning—when we met in the shop—I'd just come from the cathedral.'

'You did look bewildered.'

'How did you find out . . . that I'd left?'

'I heard—from Melanie Carter, as a matter of fact.'

'Do you know her?'

'Yes. Not very well.'

'And Theresa?'

'Yes. I know all about that.' (Smile.)

'It was the most stupid thing I've ever done,' Dawson said, and he drank some more of his whisky.

'Oh really,' Jenny said, 'I hope you don't worry about it.'

'Is she all right?'

'She's got very thin—a bit too thin, really, but otherwise she's all right.'

'What are you going to do now?' she asked.

'I'm already a journalist,' he said.

'That's quick.'

'I've got a job on the *Beaconsfield Gazette*.'

'The *Beaconsfield Gazette*? What on earth's that?'

'I got it through a school friend . . . Bobby Winterman.'

'Ah, Bobby . . . He's a friend of yours, is he?'

'Yes. Do you know him?'

'Mmm . . .' She started to laugh. 'What a funny friend for you to have.'

'I couldn't have done without him.'

'Did you tell him you were coming to see me?'

'No. I haven't seen him for a week or two.'

'He certainly is a useful friend—but I must say, it throws new light on both of you.'

'What sort of light?'

'I don't know. To your credit, I'd say.'

Jenny stood up and went to put her empty glass down on the tray.

'It's rather a coincidence,' Dawson said, 'that you know both the Carters and Bobby.'

'Not really. You'll find that everyone knows everyone else.'

'How did you meet them?'

'I've known Bobby for a long time . . . since Oxford, I think. Melanie Carter and I met on the committee of a Charity Ball. That was in my Catholic days.'

'Are they over?'

'Of course,' she said.

They went down to the kitchen which was on the ground floor next to the panelled hall-way. Two children, the little girl who had opened the door and a boy who was slightly older, sat in front of crusts of bread and empty eggshells watching television. A sharp-faced, middle-aged woman stood up as they came in.

'Nanny,' said Jenny, 'this is Mr Dawson. Henny, Mark, say hello and then up you go to bed.'

The children, Mark and Henrietta, said hello without removing their eyes from the television set. But the nanny switched it off, cleared their plates from the table and took the children upstairs.

'I hope you don't mind a simple dinner,' Jenny said, and she started to boil some water for the French beans that had been already prepared and left on the sideboard.

'Of course not. Anything.'

'Would you open some wine?' she asked Dawson, handing him a bottle and a corkscrew. He did so, filling two glasses, handing one to her at the stove as she fried veal in butter and lemon.

'You know,' she said, 'I'm sure you could do better than the *Beaconsfield Gazette*.'

'One's got to begin somewhere.'

'Yes, but . . . goodness, you're twice as intelligent as most journalists. And what you've been through, it's much more the sort of experience that gives you real understanding than five years as a cub reporter in Manchester or something like that.'

'I don't know.'

'If Bobby can't do better, I'll introduce you to Tom.'

'Who's he?'

'He's on *The Times*. Or there's Teddy Hopkins on the *Mail*. I don't know him well, but we could easily get him round to dinner some time.'

'I'm not particularly ambitious,' Dawson said.

'No, of course not, but you'd like the best job you can get, wouldn't you?'

She brought over what she had cooked—the veal in its sauce, the French beans, some wild rice, garlic bread and salad. She lit three candles and turned out the electric light. 'I hope you don't think it's phoney—a candle-lit dinner in the kitchen,' she said with a smile.

'Not at all,' said Dawson. 'It's very nice.'

'It's better than electric light.'

'I'm very impressed with your . . . your competence.'

'I'm old for my years,' she said, 'but then I was married for nearly seven of them.'

'You were very young.'

'Yes,' she said, 'like you. And now we've both grown up at last.'

The next time Dawson went to see Jenny Stanten, there were five other people there, all half-drunk, talking loudly, making jokes. Only one of them was a woman and she was ignored by her husband who, like the other men, directed all his remarks to Jenny, competing for her attention. Dawson was introduced to them. 'Ah, the monk, the monk,' one shouted (Henry Poll) and they all laughed.

They were sitting in the kitchen when he arrived and he sat down with them but kept out of the conversation. He, Jenny and the wife were the only ones to listen to it, for every rhetorical questions from one man was answered by a diversionary question; and every anecdote was sabotaged before the punch-line by the beginning of another. Dawson, sheltered for so long, was astonished at the way in which the four men ignored and interrupted each other, laughing only in return for a laugh. Jenny, aware that the buffoonery was for her benefit, smiled and graciously served out more wine, whisky and *moussaka*.

'It was Jo Hounslow, and do you know what he had the gall to say?'

'I remember when Jo used to . . .'

'I dare say he wanted to know what the hell you were doing in your bedroom at that time of day . . .'

The shouting continued for the entire evening. Dawson was ignored in the way that actors ignore the audience in the cheaper seats. There was one moment when one of the men took Dawson aside.

'I'm most interested in what you've done,' he said quietly. 'Is there a chance that you might write a book about it?'

'I don't think so,' Dawson said.

'A pity. There's a demand for that kind of book, you know, especially in America.'

'Are you a publisher?'

'That's right.'

'What sort of book do you mean?'

'I don't know. Anything you like. Think it over. I could probably offer you seven or eight hundred pounds advance, if that would be an inducement.' Then the publisher went back to his seat at the table and once again joined in the shouting chit-chat.

Later in the evening Jenny came over to Dawson, sitting silent at the periphery of the circle. She talked to him about nothing in particular but in an apologetic tone. The four others continued their banter but it faltered as they saved their best stories and jokes for Jenny's return. It came about soon enough and Dawson left at ten.

All this optimism over Jenny Stanten and her circle of friends was dissipated by this one evening. Why did someone who had seemed so sympathetic surround herself with such men? Or had she, like Penelope, no control over her suitors? In any case, there was little value in her friendship if it was as cheap as this, and he made no attempt to see her again.

Five days later, in Beaconsfield, while he was planning the lay-out of the sports page, Jenny Stanten appeared in his office at the *Gazette*.

'I thought there might be a chance that you'd be free for lunch,' she said. She looked at him, half-timid, half-smiling. They went out into Beaconsfield and found a genteel restaurant which provided a three-course lunch for six and sixpence per person.

'I'm sorry about the other evening,' she said.

'No . . . I didn't behave very well, I'm afraid.'

'I didn't realize what bores they all are until . . . well, until

I saw them with you.'

'I wasn't very amusing.'

'I think you're the only person I know who says something only if its worth saying.'

The other people in the restaurant, respectable, middle-aged ladies, stared surreptitiously at the beautifully dressed young woman and the pale, thin young man.

'I'm sure you don't realize,' Jenny said, 'how weak and empty most people are.'

Dawson laughed. 'I've heard their confessions.'

'Yes, but that must give a false impression of them. After all, if they're worried about right and wrong, that makes them seem deep, in a way. In fact, they're nothing.'

'There must be something to those . . . I mean, if they're friends of yours.'

'I'll tell you what there is. Four of them want to sleep with me and Benji doesn't only because he's queer: and he'd like to marry me because he likes the house and the children and the money.'

'Why do you see them?'

'I've got to see someone. I'm not a nun,' and she laughed and Dawson laughed after her, both without effort.

'Aren't you in love with anyone?' Dawson asked.

'It's not as easy as you think,' she said darkly. That is to say, she said it in that changed tone of voice—lower and slower—which any human being could understand to denote more meaning than the simple words.

Jenny Stanten

She was born in Aldershot in 1943. Her father was then a Company Quarter-Master Sergeant but was later promoted from the ranks to hold a King's Commission. By the end of the Second World War he was a colonel in the Royal Signals. In 1948 he retired and went to live in Bury St Edmunds, Suffolk.

Jenny went to a private school which specialized in the daughters of army officers. When she was thirteen her contemporaries discovered that her father had risen from the ranks: theirs, of course, had all been officer cadets at Sandhurst. Henceforth her friends Maud and Elizabeth would not be seen with her. Only Christine, whose father had also risen from the ranks, would be her friend—which was humiliation enough in itself.

Her father, the colonel, wished that he had had a son, and disciplined his daughter with a belt until her first menstrual period when her mother intervened and the belt was spared. At sixteen she ran away from home and reached London. At this age she remained a gawky adolescent: no one could guess at her future beauty. This fact, and the rules of the house in which she found a room, preserved her virginity for the time being. Jenny worked in a shop in Croydon. Her landlady made sure that she gave up most of her wages for board and lodging. She was teased by the delivery boys but only went out with the other girls.

Four months later she returned home. Her parents said nothing. Her mother once remarked that tampons were unhealthy and then burst into tears. Her father, now old, picked at the hard skin on his hands.

A friend of the colonel's wife advised that they send Jenny to a tutorial establishment in Oxford where she could catch up on the work she had missed at school. Jenny herself liked the idea and her parents complied—happy to be rid of her morose presence and eager to get back to their garden. Thus it was that she went to this university town.

The tutorial establishment had no direct connection with Oxford University. It taught the daughters of the rich and moderately rich anything from Advanced Level English to typing and shorthand. Jenny made several friends among the others girls and was asked to parties given by undergraduates in the different colleges. From her girl-friends she learnt to dress well in metropolitan style: and in these nice clothes, her beauty at last came into its own.

Its most obvious aspect was the length, slenderness and shaping of her legs. Her face, as we know, was lovely enough and could express warmth and humour most prettily. She had that quality of seeming amused and interested when she was deeply bored: but it was the tripping limbs hinged to her hips which first caught the eye. They acted, as it were, as rails on which a glance would be carried past normal, not exceptional, waist and bust to the more refined organs of the head. Her hands were delicate and her finger-nails well kept. Her feet, of course, were blistered by the kind of shoes she wore, but no one was likely to notice them if there was anything to be seen of her legs.

It was here, at Oxford, that she met Matthew Stanten. He had long, blond hair which curled nicely over his collar and was thought brilliant. His success at Oxford was aided by his age. He had done his National Service in the army and so was three years older than most of the other undergraduates. He had a reputation with women. While most students edged into awkward relationships with equally ham-handed girls, he was known to go all the way and at once. In other words he was considered an adult in a community where this was a prestigious thing to be.

He was also very rich. His father had died in his first year at Oxford leaving him half a million in stocks, bonds and real estate. His mother had long since been divorced from her husband and lived in Cannes. The day after his father's funeral, Matthew had bought an Austin-Healey sports car and had wrecked it on a municipal lamp-post within a week. When Jenny appeared, he was in his last year and his car was an Alfa-Romeo.

Matthew saw Jenny on the street in Oxford and noticed only her legs in the casual, lecherous way he had noticed a dozen others. Later, however, when she was talked about as the prettiest and most amusing girl around, the Zuleika Dobson of that academic year, he found out who knew her, arranged a meeting and later asked her to lunch. Jenny also knew about Matthew: the other girls told her of his eligibility and openly envied her the date.

She came to Matthew's lodgings to have lunch. He was wearing jeans that creased at the crotch, and he set about making a Savoyard omelette, talking all the time as he did so. Outside: a summer sun, a leisurely students' day of odd lectures, coffee bars and casual introductions to contemporaries from all over the country.

'In Aden, actually, I had a servant,' he said.

Jenny dangled her legs, one crossed over the other. She was wearing a purple jersey and blue skirt, the smartest of her casual clothes. She sat quite aware of them.

'Can you cook?' asked Matthew.

'No,' she said.

They ate the omelette and drank vintage Burgundy. Matthew heated bread in front of the fire—there were odd plates and forks, odd cups for coffee. Jenny sat on the bed: Matthew sat on the floor. For her it was unbelievable freedom —to be alone behind a closed door with another, alone on the inner side of that door. She made no offer to wash the plates. She listened to Matthew talk and she smiled at the calculation behind the topics—love affairs, travel, good hotels, good food. She might have been giving off an addictive odour for the way he hovered and concentrated on her presence. She moved to feel the clothes against her skin.

They went to a film. They came back. She had no doubts in her mind as to what would happen. It was a summer afternoon which stayed light. Jenny took off her coat and stood facing the mantel, studying the invitations and fixtures placed against the wall. Matthew turned her and embraced her, his hands under her purple jersey. He undressed her and seduced her as he had the officers' wives and the Scandinavian girls from the language schools at Oxford.

The account of her parents which she gave to her lover so horrified him that he felt for her as for a fellow orphan. When they married, it was with only two friends present. Matthew took her on a honeymoon around the world which lasted for three months. Then they came back to the houses he had inherited—one in Northamptonshire, the other in Chelsea.

Since he had been awarded a first class degree, Matthew was offered several jobs—in ministries, in merchant banks: but he had a large income from dividends and saw no point in taking a job at once, though all agreed that he should do something sometime. So this couple spent their time entertaining and being entertained, travelling abroad, spending their week-ends in their country house, buying and furnishing and then selling an old castle in Ireland. Jenny bought clothes and two pug puppies. She had her first child. She was by then just nineteen.

Matthew, like most of his friends, joined Crockford's and gambled once or twice a week, often until seven the next morning. He then spent more nights of the week away from the house in Cheyne Row, not to gamble, as Jenny thought, but to make love with the wife of a friend.

Jenny told her husband that one or two of his friends had proposed love affairs to her. He told her to ignore them, which she did. The ardour of some of them was only increased. Two declared their love for her and one was so enthusiastic that he told her of Matthew's infidelity. Jenny asked him if it was true. 'Good heavens, Jenny,' he said. 'Did you expect me to be faithful for ever?'

'Yes,' she said.

'That's very Bury St Edmunds,' he said and laughed and patted her on the buttocks.

Six months later, Jenny had her first affair with—Alexis

Bornodov, a kind, handsome portrait painter, ten years older than she was.

She wanted to leave Matthew for Alexis, but unfortunately Alexis had only what he earned from the rich, or was given by his wife who was one of them. And when this wife found out about her husband's latest girl, he was forced to give the girl up, though with the tact and consideration for which he was so well known.

Matthew, too, had a different mistress.

Since falling in love with Alexis, Jenny had found her husband repugnant, but he still insisted on sleeping with her when he was at home. This random impregnation was the way of things in London, if not in Bury St Edmunds. She bore a second child.

Jenny was told that Alexis had taken on another girl. She distracted herself by sacking the nurse-maid and taking care of the children herself. Some months later, when Matthew was away shooting in Scotland, a friend of his called Jack came round to the house in Cheyne Row. It was eleven o'clock on a Saturday night. Jenny was in her dressing-gown, ready for bed, and Jack made himself ready too by stripping off all his clothes in front of her. Not wishing to wake the children ... or for some other reason, Jenny took her second lover. Next morning Jack went to mass down the street at the Church of Saint Thomas More. His family had been Catholic since before the Reformation. He came back for lunch and stayed: he remained, in fact, until Matthew came back, when he retired to a safer distance to live and fight again another day.

This Recusant made a strong impression on Jenny, if only for hurrying his sperm-smeared body to church that Sunday morning. She took to going to mass, under his influence, first to this church, then to the cathedral. Matthew encouraged her religious mood, being unaware of its real source, and unable to stop its inevitable impetus, she was first instructed and then baptized by a young priest at the Cathedral—Father Dawson.

Her husband was unaffected by her religiosity. He gambled more. He drank more. He got up late and went to bed in the early morning. Jack, the Recusant, moved on. Jenny thought of leaving Matthew but knew she could only return penniless to Bury St Edmunds. At one point, she pretended to leave him. She persuaded Benji to go with her but left a clear enough trail. Matthew followed them and found them and, being drunk, beat them both. With the same spirit that had led her to run away from home at fourteen, at twenty-four she thought of killing Matthew, of pushing him over the parapet of the castle in Ireland—but then they sold the castle and another occasion never arose.

And then, arriving home with his wife from a party in Sussex, Matthew Stanten drove the car into a tree and was killed when the steering-wheel pierced his breast.

Beaconsfield: the statue of Disraeli, the neo-classical brick buildings.

'Have you ever loved anyone, besides your husband?' Dawson asked Jenny.

'No . . . well, there were one or two I thought I loved, as I thought I loved Matthew, once, so the answer is either yes, I've been in love two or three times, or no, I've never been in love. Or I don't know what love is. And you?' she asked Dawson.

'Me?'

'Have you ever been in love?'

'No.'

'Not even with Theresa Carter?' She asked this almost with a sneer.

'No.'

Jenny changed her tone (to slow and soft). 'That's sad . . . sad for you.'

'Yes. I suppose it is.'

They came out of the restaurant into the wide, light street.

'Would you come to the house again some time?' she asked. 'I promise there'll be no one else there.'

'Yes, even . . .'

'The only people I want you to meet are those who might help you get a new job. You don't want to spend the rest of your life here . . .' She made a gesture of contempt for Beaconsfield.

'It's really not so bad,' said Dawson.

She gave him another of her direct glances. 'Perhaps I'm being very insensitive, interfering like this. Perhaps you find me just as boring as my friends.'

'Of course not,' Dawson said. 'And it isn't just a matter of being interesting.'

'No, you're right.'

'When can I come?'

'Come tomorrow.'

Kissing her went well enough, but when Dawson started to undo the buttons of her blouse his hands shook so much that the delicate task became impossible. Jenny looked at him in the eyes to see what was wrong, and was reassured to see that he was not biting his tongue or frothing at the mouth. She laid her hand on his at her bosom and held him, shaking, with her other arm.

'I'm sorry,' he said.

'Really,' she said, 'you mustn't worry.'

They lay still on the sofa and the shaking subsided, but so did the desire. Dawson sat up.

'Don't go,' Jenny said. 'You mustn't go.'

That night, then, Dawson slept in the spare room of the house in Cheyne Row. When he woke up at eight, Jenny was sitting on his bed looking into his face.

'I'll make you some breakfast,' she said.

Dawson came back to Cheyne Row the next evening and talked to the two children while they ate their supper. Henrietta was aggressive and impudent, taunting him, seeming to know that he would only humour her. The son, Mark, sat shovelling cereal into his mouth, the inherited fatness of his chin and neck moving solemnly with his jaws, his eyes as cold and languorous as those of a hanging judge.

Dawson and the children's mother then went to a film on the King's Road—*The Guns of Navarone*. He held her hand throughout and afterwards went back with her to her home. They sat in the kitchen eating sandwiches without appetite. Then they went up to her bedroom.

'Look,' she said, holding up a pair of dark blue pyjamas, 'I bought these for you.'

Her room was at the front of the house: her dressing-room and bathroom at the back. The three were connected to each other through the dressing-room. The bedroom itself was long and narrow: her large bed filled almost half of it. There was a thick brown carpet covering the floor and brown silk curtains and bedspread. The same carpet continued through the dressing-room. The bathroom floor was also carpeted, but in blue. The bath and basin were old-fashioned and ornate, one with lion's-paw legs, the other with a curved stand. There was an oval mirror above the basin.

'My darling,' she said, placing her hand on his cheek. Then she turned away. 'Do you want a bath or anything?' she asked.

'No, I had one this morning.'

'Oh yes.'

'But you have one if you want.'

'No, I had one earlier on.'

Dawson went back into the bedroom while Jenny started to wash her face and hands and brush her teeth. He changed into the pyjamas, putting his clothes on a chair. Then he went back into the bathroom. Jenny was in her nightdress which was of white cotton, came down to her ankles and had lace around the neck.

'It's all yours,' she said pointing to the basin. She picked up a blue toothbrush. 'I even bought you this,' she said, and smiled.

Dawson smiled too and took it from her. She left him then and he brushed his teeth and washed his face and hands and his feet in the bath, studying the row of creams, lotions and powders on the shelf behind it. When he came back into the bedroom, Jenny was in bed, lying well to one side of it, reading a book. He got in beside her. She closed her book.

'We'll go to sleep, don't you think?'

'Yes,' he said.

Jenny turned off the light. 'Good night,' she said. He said the same and they both lay down, facing out. But Dawson was accustomed to sleep on the other side of his body, so after a few minutes he turned over. He became drowsy but did not sleep. She breathed regularly, but he did not feel that she was asleep either. He felt the warmth of her body from across the bed and moved closer to it with a movement disguised as a mere settling of his body on the mattress. Her knees were drawn up towards her chin, so it was her buttocks which touched him on his stomach. It occurred to him only then that she was probably naked under her cotton nightdress. Involuntarily, he drew back, but then relaxed and felt his stomach touch her again. He fancied that her breathing was now less regular but she kept quite still. Within him there was a strange battle of will and instinct: on the one hand he encouraged his instinct to manifest itself, which it did; on the other, he tried to suppress his timidity and force himself to make some move. He put his arms around her waist, his lower arm burrowing between her body and the mattress. There again he hesitated, terrified of what she might feel touching her through pyjamas and nightdress. But then she turned towards him and took his head in her hands, kissing his lips and murmuring incoherent words. He returned her kisses, but she must have sensed that the lower half of his body was keeping its distance, for her hands came down from his head to his loins and drew them to hers so that all misgivings had to be abandoned, and will and instinct became less and less distinct until, after further guiding gestures, their actions had an impetus all of their own.

Nine

There were and there still are a selection of the richest, best looking and most intelligent men in London who would greatly have envied Dawson his position in Jenny Stanten's house, heart, bed, etc. No one quite knows who taught her what she knew (Bordonov, perhaps, or even Matthew Stanten himself), she had acquired a reputation for expertness and originality that, taken with her beauty, would drive the most lackadaisical admirer to a high pitch of fervour. She turned most of them down, of course, and no passion is so great that it cannot find some satisfaction elsewhere: yet the most detached must have felt some chagrin when it became evident that she had chosen Eddie Dawson, the monk, over all of them.

One might think that Dawson was lucky to have his first experiences in this field from such an expert, but misfortune of a sort came into this as into everything else. So besotted were his emotions with love, that he was never able to appreciate the play of his senses. For from what he told me, he had no consciousness and no memory of making love with Jenny. It was just an expression of a sentiment. When he was with her in these early days his eyes were always on her eyes, his tall body stooping not with lust but with solicitude—his thin face set in a smile of surprise at this unexpected fulfilment.

There now followed months of pleasant life for both of them—a home and happiness in each other. They had different reasons for loving one another, and the reasons may not have been good ones, but as likely as not they never are. The only evidence at this time that this might have been so was for both of them the slight embarrassment they felt when either gave their reasons for loving the other. She said: 'You're the only man I've ever met with the strength of mind to take his life into his own hands and change it to the way he wants it to be.' He said: 'I feel like a seed that's just been planted. Really, you have the natural kindness of the soil.'

Now Dawson was not aware of his will, and Jenny had never thought of herself as earth, but both were able to put aside these awkward feelings and smile at each other and enjoy their love.

Dawson gave up his flat and moved into Cheyne Row with his few belongings. He continued to work on the *Gazette* for a time: but then, through a friend of Jenny's, he was offered a series on a Fleet Street paper. He talked to me before he signed the contract, first to say that he would be giving up the job I had found for him, and then to ask for my advice. He was to write a series of twelve articles: for each he would be paid one hundred and fifty pounds. I asked if they had suggested any particular topic. He said that the first was to be on the Catholic Church. I knew that this paper was capable of surreptitious sensationalism so I asked if they had mentioned any line of publicity for the series.

'Well,' he said, 'they want to say something about my past, of course. The by-line will be Monk Dawson.'

'Are you going to let them do that?'

'Yes, I mean, I don't see why not. There's no point in hiding it.'

He behaved as if nothing, now, could affect his happiness and so I left it at that. He would make less money, of course, but Jenny had evidently made it clear that he would have no concerns of that sort. Matthew Stanten had left seven hundred thousand pounds and she was free to do what she liked with the income. She certainly made good use of it. I had lunch with Dawson every now and then and he began to appear in well-cut suits and silk shirts: and often he would mention that they had just come back from Paris or the South of France.

In summer he went with Jenny and the children to their home in Northamptonshire. It was a large house with an estate of a thousand acres attached to it. The buildings were not more than seventy-five years old, and because of the period of its construction, the house was solid and ugly. The servants here were paid for out of a separate trust which existed for the two children.

The countryside had meagre undulations: there was never a clear view over more than two or three fields. Because the family came rarely, there were no neighbours on whom they might call or who would visit them. A separate bedroom had been prepared for Dawson and his suitcase was unpacked for him. Jenny came into this bedroom, having changed into a long skirt for the evening.

'I hate this place,' she said, 'but we have to come here at least once a year . . . and the children adore it.'

They went down to dinner which was served to them by the butler. Dawson made an attempt to talk and behave as they usually did when eating together, but Jenny on this first evening seemed preoccupied with sitting up straight. They moved from the dining-room into the billiard room which had a full-sized table in good condition. While Jenny read a fashion magazine she had brought from London, Dawson knocked three balls together, setting one after the other, sharp and fast, over the baize to the cushion, watching them bounce, collide and ricochet. Coffee was brought to them.

They went to bed early. 'Will you come to my room?' Jenny whispered when they had reached the top of the stairs. They parted then and went in different directions down the landing. Dawson washed and changed into his pyjamas and dressing-gown. He then walked back down the landing. The lights had been turned out. He found Jenny's room in the obscurity. It was the master bedroom. All the furniture had been carved in mock medieval style at the turn of the century. The ceiling was high, dark blue and broken by plaster stalactites. In the same style, the windows were narrow and pointed with lead frames.

Jenny sat at a dressing table. As Dawson came in she made a face as if to say that the moment was awful and fun, both together. Dawson had been annoyed by the sleeping arrangements, but Jenny seemed to find them amusing.

'It's like having a midnight feast, or something,' she said.

'I suppose I'll have to creep back to my bedroom at four in the morning,' said Dawson.

'Oh darling, I am sorry, I know, it's awful, but I just couldn't face the atmosphere, you know, Mr and Mrs Muster —if they knew.'

'I'm sure they do know.'

'Yes, of course, but there are conventions, even about adultery.'

'I don't look on it as adultery.'

'No. I'm sorry. Please don't get cross. It's so gloomy here anyway.'

They then lifted themselves into the large bed and lay between the cold, stiff sheets, hugging each other like the babes in the wood: and in this position they fell asleep, one body accustomed to the twitches and breathing of the other.

Much of each day in Northamptonshire was spent with the two children. They showed no particular love for Dawson and though he was committed as we all are to loving them, in secret he detested them. Mark who was eight or nine had the round pompous face of a country gentleman which went well with the house and the landscape. He was coldly civil to all, but preferred the company of the butler and housekeeper, being already aware of their deference. Henrietta was more like her mother and seemed to compete with her for Dawson's attention by gross flirtation that amounted to exhibitionism, a flaunting of private parts and provoking of dirty talk.

In the evening, and for certain parts of the day, the children were taken in charge by the woman who was paid to look after them. Then the mother and her lover would discover how little there is to do in the country unless you are adept at its pursuits. Humble folk grow vegetables and are happy to stroll in the fields, but here the facilities were for hunting foxes and shooting birds.

'It's all such nonsense, isn't it?' Jenny said to Dawson, the guest in her heart and the home of her dead husband. And he, politely replied: 'Oh no, it's a good life, in a way.'

'Then . . . would you like to ride?' she asked. 'I do, sometimes.'

'Yes,' he said (politely).

Confusing love and hospitality, Dawson did not say that he had never ridden before. He was put on a quiet horse but when it trotted, he was jogged on its back, not knowing the way of rising in the saddle. This shook his kidneys and bruised his balls—but any pain could be suffered for love. Jenny, who had a good seat, looked back from her cantering mare and, seeing Dawson like a comic squire on a mule, reined in.

'Haven't you ridden before?' she asked.

'Not really,' he said, straining to keep his balance on the bored horse.

'You should rise like this,' she said, lifting her butt from the saddle on the legs she had squeezed at his throat. And in pain instead of delight he learnt another art from his mistress which she taught with less patience and less pleasure.

In the evenings, they would talk. Was it not, after all, intellectual sympathy that had founded their love?

'Do you think one can speak in terms of maturity of mankind,' Jenny asked, 'as one does of an individual's maturity?'

'I think so, don't you? There is some kind of communal wisdom which . . . well, for example, one could say that, by and large, we are more humane than we used to be.'

'Yes.'

'And if we can comprehend, with our reason, the allegorical truths of religion—that would be a new maturity.'

This kind of talk. Jenny would ask questions as a pupil to a teacher: 'Why is it,' she once asked, 'that people live in so much confusion, not knowing what to do with their lives?'

'I think the only explanation is an ethological one: that at an early state of evolution, the human being needed this anguish, a sort of guilt about living, to foster feelings of social obligation which kept the tribe together and at peace with itself.'

'Yes, I see. And now?'

'And now we no longer need the taboos because we understand, rationally, the nature of society. Intuition is redundant.'

'It is an exciting time to live in, isn't it?' Jenny said.

'As you say—the maturity of man.'

'But what's to be done about people who don't see all this?'

'Inevitably, there are individuals who lag behind the communal level of understanding. Religion has some function for them, I suppose.'

'I think Matthew would have been better off with a religion . . .'

'Possibly.'

Jenny got up from sitting on the rug in front of the fire. 'Oh darling,' she said, interposing her body between his and the arm of the ample chair, 'how I've longed for someone to talk to and to explain things to me like this. I had such a rotten education.'

'You help me to think things out,' Dawson said, taking her in his arms and kissing her face, her eyes, her nose. 'You give me ideas for those articles I'm supposed to be writing.'

Jenny had one habit, one mannerism, which embarrassed,

ven irritated Dawson. While she had shown a certain awe before the butler, she was contemptuous of people in shops, people on either side of the counter. When entering a shop, she would put on a fixed, beatific smile and walk to the front of the queue, interrupt a customer in the middle of his order and demand her own. Now the English are a particularly fair people and are acutely pained when anyone breaks the rules like this. Dawson shared their agony. He shared the confusion of the milliners and confectioners and chemists when they were confronted with such arrogant intrusion from this blithe girl. If they knew her, and knew how rich she was, they humoured her: but on the whole they reacted stubbornly and either ignored her or told her to wait her turn. This she would do as if herself humouring the crass side of the human soul.

When Dawson felt he knew her well enough, he remarked on this habit of hers.

'Oh, they're all such fools,' she said.

'But you never even wait your turn.'

'They should have more people to serve. They take enough of my money, after all. I don't want to spend my whole life waiting in shops.'

She showed a trace of the same irritation talking about it, but then she smiled and said she would try to remember to be more patient and polite—for his sake.

On the journey back from Northamptonshire, there was a grotesque incident of this sort. With the two children and the nanny they stopped at a restaurant for tea. Jenny liked her tea without milk or sugar and, since it was served by the cup, she asked the waitress to make this exception. The waitress forgot and brought her a cup with milk and sugar already in it. Jenny was incensed (they were all tired and thirsty) and called the waitress a stupid bitch. The waitress, a slow girl, started to cry. So did the children. The manager came to the scene and Jenny berated him for the stupidity of the waitress. Dawson tried to calm her down but she ignored him. In the end they all left without having had anything to drink.

No one said a word until they reached London. Then the children were fed and sent to bed. Jenny ordered the nurse to make supper and then went upstairs to the drawing-room. The nurse complained to Dawson that it was not part of her duties to cook for them. Dawson therefore made an omelette for himself and Jenny. He called her down from the drawing-room. Neither spoke while they ate it. Dawson leant across to fill her glass with wine and in doing so, spilt some of it on the table. In a quick, concentrated gesture, she picked up the glass and threw it on the floor. Her eyes, while she did so, were fixed on Dawson. He lifted his hand to hit her, but then let it fall to the table. 'What on earth's the matter?' he asked. Jenny continued to stare at him, defiantly, but his expression was now unmistakably perplexed, and not angry. Thus she subsided and explained that she sometimes had these moods.

'You really must just beat me down,' she said.

'No, if you want to behave like that . . .'

'No, I don't, really I don't. But I need someone else to control me. It's like hysterics. You needn't be afraid of hurting me, I mean, to bring me to my senses.'

Of course Dawson was always able to control himself and he never struck her in anger: in fact he never struck her at all. It must have been self-discipline of his earlier life, because Jenny gave him frequent excuses for doing so.

Dawson's first article, in its original form, was a reasoned piece on why he felt people no longer needed religion. He mentioned the girl who was seduced by her father and told of other innocent sins, juxtaposing them with the sinful self-righteousness of most Christians. The evils of this world were social, not theological. The extirpation of them was a task for Man, not God.

He had sent in this article from Northamptonshire and when he got back to London he went to Fleet Street to see the friend of Jenny's who had commissioned it. This was neither Sam nor Harry but a man called David Allenby. He was a professional journalist, perpetually in shirt-sleeves, committed to the public image of a journalist as she was committed to the public image of everything. He was balding, middle-aged, divorced, a heavy drinker, a heavy smoker, lecherous and only on the fringe of Jenny's circle of friends. He was good at his job and was thought to be responsible for raising the circulation of his paper at a time when many others were closing down.

In contrast to the grandiose entrance to the newspaper, the office of David Allenby, its assistant editor, was small and sweaty.

'This is fine, Edward, just fine,' said Allenby. 'Coffee, Sue, yes?'

'Is it all right?'

'Fine. There's one thing, though,' he said, turning over the pages which Dawson recognized as those he had written. 'I'd like to see just a bit more of the personal stuff . . .'

'I know,' said Dawson. 'The snag there is . . . well, there isn't much of a personal side to a priest's life.'

'Yes, I see that—the organization takes over?'

'Exactly.'

'But . . . you see, what the reader will be asking, since you were an R.C. priest, is about this thing of sex.'

'Well . . .'

'The unnatural demands of celibacy—something like that.'

'That really wasn't a problem.'

The assistant editor's face, lean from the exercise it took in making many different expressions, now strained to keep its position of good humour; and this effort was noticeable in the tone of his voice.

'Really, no problem? I mean to say, I know several people who have been after Jenny Stanten for years and then you go and scoop us all.'

'I didn't leave the priesthood for Jenny.'

'But she confessed to you, didn't she?'

'Yes. But that was before . . .'

'While you were still a priest, I assume?'

'Yes, but it was a coincidence.'

'Come off it,' said David Allenby. 'You don't get your cock up a skirt like that if it's been doing a Rip van Winkle for twenty years.'

'Really,' Dawson said again, his face reddening, his voice rising, 'it wasn't a problem.'

'Look,' said Allenby, his facial muscles finally relaxing into an expression of envy and distaste, 'I don't want to hear about what went on with the choir boys behind the altar, but we've got to have something that'll cover the sex angle because our readers think about it and sweat about it and they don't want to read about someone who says he can do without it.'

Hence a paragraph on the loneliness of being a priest was provided by Monk Dawson, and a phrase or two was inserted about the lack of feminine companionship and affection, and how this was felt most acutely on sleepless nights . . . and it was a paragraph he wrote with some feeling because he did now know the delight of returning to a home and a woman who cared about what he had done that day and was happy to have him back. And in this pleasant atmosphere he proceeded to write further articles about more specific social problems and their humanistic solution.

The material for these articles he gathered in the police stations and law courts—and the other various public institutions which exist to force society on unsocial human beings. On one day he would go to a press conference at the Home Office, the next to the Divorce courts, the day after that to a home or hospital. Each institution was a building and within each building there were offices with files on the petty tragedies that came before them: and sometimes the people were drawn to their file, out from the many millions, there to act out a certain phase in their case which would become a page or paragraph in the file.

Dawson would talk to them—prostitute, thief, patient, or discriminatory landlord. He was too good a journalist to preach to them: but he would listen with his own formula like a matrix to catch the molten metal of their bitterness and abuse. Not to their face would he answer them—would he dispel their despair—but in his paper a week or so later they could read if they wished the solution to their misfortunes. He wrote, and he wished us all to act, as if men and women were fundamentally good; as if the only evil were to doubt this and cynically cater for wickedness. Thus he was a true and good liberal—as unhappy about the existence of the police as of criminals. Instinctively, also, he favoured the wretched over the righteous and reserved his deepest sympathy for them—which was what eventually destroyed his own righteousness: for it became quite apparent that most criminals did not regard themselves as wretched but merely unlucky. Nor did they think of good and evil or right and wrong: their lives were not open to Dawson's categories. Disaster and disruption had no moral quality about it. There was no one to thank and no one to blame.

For some time Dawson was unaffected by their attitude, but when he started to work on his article on orphans his judging mind was momentarily confounded. 'The trouble here, Mr Dawson,' the matron said to him, 'is that half of our hard-core children are coloured, and they're almost impossible to place with foster parents. An English parent is usually quite reluctant, you see, to take on the additional responsibilities and we very rarely have coloured people coming here wishing to adopt. Now a Jewish child, or even a Greek or an Italian child, will be taken care of by its own community, if you see what I mean. It wouldn't even come into our hands. And there's not much difficulty in finding a home for a normal British child if he isn't too old when he comes to us.'

Her hair was in a bun. She wore a blue tunic, a white apron and the badge of the British Red Cross. Her voice was genteel and discreet: her face was covered with carelessly applied powder and lipstick.

'Of course after the coloured, the greatest problem we have is with the Irish. All these young girls come over from Ireland to have their babies, you see, to escape the scandal. But then they go back to Ireland leaving their babies with us. That wouldn't be so great a problem if they didn't always stipulate that the child must go to Catholic foster-parents. It's the law of the land, you see, that they have the right to insist on that. The mother's wishes have to be respected. Well, as you know, most Catholics have large families of their own, and they don't want to go adopting any more. And so we're left with all these lovely little children.

'I'm more sorry for the mothers, you know, than I am for the children. They're really torn apart, they are, when they leave their babies here. It's painful to watch. There's a strong instinct for the baby, you see. But they've usually made up their minds while they're pregnant. It's not just being afraid of what people will think. As often as not they think they won't get married if they've a baby; or they have to work and there's no one to leave the little thing with during the day. I really would like to tell them to keep their babies, but it's no use. They have to work it out for themselves. There's a period within which they can claim them back, but fear of one sort or another seems to be stronger than the natural instinct. They go back to their ordinary lives without their children—but they suffer terribly. It's the same if they have a termination. I knew one girl who had one and she felt quite all right afterwards until the week when the baby was to have been born. Then she went into a deep trauma. It was most extraordinary.

'Of course, we explain the use of contraceptives to them,

but it's a depressing thing for a young mother to have to think about. And to bring in a baby and exchange it for a contraceptive—it's not a fair exchange, is it? But what else can you do? What else?'

Ten

Dawson returned from the last interview to his home in Cheyne Row. The children were eating their supper with the nanny: Jenny had bathed and changed into an orange and black silk dress and was waiting for him in the drawing-room.

He sat down on the sofa and sighed.

'How did it go?' she asked, kissing him and handing him a glass of whisky and ice.

'It sometimes seems as if we are the only two happy and contented people in England.'

Jenny smiled and sat down next to him. 'There must be other men and women in love with each other.'

'I suppose so.'

'Doesn't that make them happy?'

'For a time.'

She smiled and stroked his head. 'Really, darling, what have you been doing today?'

'I went to a home for abandoned children.'

'What sort of abandoned children?'

'Bastards—one of the more regrettable by-products of love.'

'They needn't be regrettable. There must be lots of childless couples who could be made happy.'

'I'm sure there are. But it can't be very pleasant for the children to discover that they were acquired like that, to gratify some strange woman's mothering instincts. They must wonder about their real parents.'

'Nonsense,' Jenny said, drawing away from him on the sofa. 'If they don't know, it doesn't make any difference.'

'They usually find out.'

'Not necessarily.

'I should have thought that the foster parents would always tell them.'

'I don't see why.'

'Wouldn't you?'

'Henrietta wasn't Matthew's. I haven't told her.'

There was a silence. Jenny was apparently angry, with in-flamed cheeks and a fidgeting head. Dawson's jaw fell half an inch: his eyes shifted their glance around his hands and glass. 'Who's was she?' he asked.

'Well, I don't know,' she said, quiet and low. 'She could have been Matthew's but she could have been Alexis's just as easily. I was sure she was, at the time, Alexis's I mean, because I was in love with him, but perhaps it was only that. I don't know. She looks more like him.'

She was silent. Dawson stood up and went to the bottles of alcohol to create a margin of time in which the subject could be forgotten. 'You know,' he said, returning with fresh glasses of spirits for both of them, 'the more I meet these people—social misfits and so on—the less I understand the whole thing.'

'I thought you had a clear-cut explanation,' Jenny answered, turning her glass in her hand, her attention distracted from what she was saying.

'I did but—well—it doesn't seem adequate. That we should all just be content with our situation—humanistic, hedonistic and evolving. That's what I said, wasn't it? That the only problem is poverty. But, you see, all these people I've talked to are not really poor—not, at any rate, in the sense that people are poor in Asia and Africa. And even in Europe you get countries that are much poorer than ours, yet they're more stable. And America, the richest society, is probably the most chaotic.'

'Perhaps they're all just sinners,' said Jenny, still speaking in an irritated tone of voice but glancing at him to see the effect of what she had said.

'No,' Dawson said.

'What, then?'

'I don't know. Education, perhaps . . .'

'If that were true, then all our friends with their university degrees would be free from the general malaise, wouldn't they? But to judge from what you think of them, they're the worst of all.'

'Yes. It can't be education in that sense.'

'You'll have to think up some other panacea, or you won't have anything to say in your articles,' Jenny said with the final energy of her irritation.

Accepting Dawson's denigration of her friends did not lead Jenny to give them up. 'We must see some other people,' she would say: or, 'It's important for the children for us to have friends with children of the same age.' Dawson felt uncomfortable with these friends, but he had none of his own to suggest as company of a different kind. I think that I was the only friend they had in common, but Dawson preferred to see me alone and Jenny seemed embarrassed by my friendship with her lover, as if I might set him against her. Jenny understood Dawson's distaste for her usual circle of friends, and after each dinner-party or week-end in the country, she would either apologize for them or try to discover some special characteristic which might endear them to him.

'Henry really is kind, you know,' she said, speaking of Henry Poll with whom they had just been staying.

'He's so utterly negative. He doesn't do anything or stand for anything.'

'He's got a lot of money, that's all. What do you expect him to do?'

'I expect him to find some better way to amuse his guests than making them run races around his pingpong table.'

'That's just his idea of fun. He's not an intellectual.'

'I don't want him to be an intellectual. But he needn't be so futile.'

'He lent some money to Benji.'

'That can't have been much sacrifice.'

'Rich people like their money just as much as anyone else.'

'There's nothing particularly kind in being blatantly unfaithful to your wife.'

'Ah yes, well, that . . .'

Jenny would usually end such conversations by saying that Dawson did not like anyone, which seemed true enough. The only two people he would meet through choice were Demuth, an underling of Allenby's, and myself. Our friendship, as I have said before, was like the affection of two brothers who are unlike and lead different lives yet keep sight of one another. His friendship with Demuth was strange, too: this man was older and somewhat dingy in his appearance—thin, with hair flecked with white and falling out over his brow. On the other hand, he was decidedly unpretentious and to Dawson at that time it was a precious quality.

Demuth had been delegated by Allenby to deal with the articles as they came in, and writer and sub-editor would meet every ten days or so to discuss them. They might have lunch at a public house under Blackfriars Bridge or walk up Fleet Street in the evening to El Vino's.

'It's a good idea for you to do features, really,' Demuth said to Dawson. 'If you tried to get on to the staff, there might be trouble with the union. Anyway, the chances are you'd end up like me, which is hardly worth the effort, is it?'

'You haven't ended up, have you?'

'Oh yes, chum. You can tell at this stage what the prospects are—well, in any profession, for that matter.'

'What about Allenby?'

'Dave? He'll go a long way. He should do, anyway. I'll stick with him, if I can. We work well together.'

Dawson once asked Demuth back to dinner at the house. Demuth gave him a straight look after hearing this invitation. 'You live with Mrs Stanten, don't you?'

'Do you know her?'

'I know about her. Anyone who works on a paper does.'

'Why?'

'Her name used to be in the social columns two or three times a week.'

'How ridiculous. Why?'

'I don't know. She used to make that kind of news. Dave used to write the pieces for ours himself.'

'Well,' said Dawson, 'she couldn't help that.' To which Demuth did not reply.

'Why not bring your wife over and have dinner next week?' Dawson asked.

Again, the straight look. 'That's very decent of you,' Demuth said, 'but, you see, we live out at Blackheath and what with the kids and all that, it's just too complicated for the wife to come in. I'd like to come, though, if that'd be all right.'

He went back with Dawson that evening. Dawson was irritated because Jenny became artificially gracious, asking incessant questions about his work when he, Dawson, knew quite well that she had no interest in it. In fact she never let up so Dawson had no chance to talk to his guest himself.

Demuth stood up to go quite early in the evening, saying that he had to catch a train back to Blackheath. Dawson took him to the door.

'Thanks,' Demuth said, 'I enjoyed that. You've a nice set-up here, really, a nice set-up.' He then walked away and after that they only ever met in the bars on Fleet Street.

One wonders why Jenny and Edward did not get married. I never could bring myself to ask Dawson outright, but I once skirted around the subject by mentioning my own desire to have children. 'But one needs a mother,' I said, 'and I can't seem to find the right girl.'

'I know,' he said, 'I know the feeling, but I'd like to be sure of what to teach the child before I brought him into the world. One can provide a material home easily enough, but there ought to be a philosophical one, don't you think?'

'Perhaps. But I thought you knew, anyway.'

'Knew what?'

'Well, the answers. I thought you had a philosophy of life.'

'Yes, I have, but it isn't tested.'

'Don't leave it too late.'

Dawson smiled. 'We're both quite young still, aren't we? So is Jenny—though she has her children, of course.'

'Doesn't she want a child of yours?'

'I don't know. She takes the pill so she can't want one just now. She may be a little afraid of marrying again, since her first marriage was such a mistake.'

'Yes.'

'And as she says, things are so perfect as they are.'

Indeed they were perfect. They still talked together as much as before, even if Dawson's side of the conversation became less authoritative. Jenny, in the role of his pupil, would invade these areas of his uncertainty as the Cossacks harried the Grand Army.

'You used to say that we should overcome our primitive guilt over living, isn't that right?'

'Yes.'

'Isn't social conscience simply part of guilt for living?'

'Not. It's sympathy, not guilt.'

'But isn't sympathy perhaps a hangover from an earlier phase of evolution? I mean—why sympathize with others?'

'Why? Because we're fellow human beings.'

'Yes, but . . . I mean I don't want to become a bore about

it, but why should fellow human beings care a damn about one another? This awful phoney sorrow that comes over people when there's an earthquake or something, and a few hundred get killed. One doesn't go into a panic over the thousands who die of old age: it's only when we're afraid that our lives might end like that—cancer or on the roads. Sympathy is just fear at one remove, isn't it?'

'Yes, well,' said Dawson, 'there's a lot of truth in that.'

On another occasion: 'You only really dislike my friends because they're rich, don't you?' she asked.

'Perhaps . . .'

'That's prejudice, isn't it?'

'People who are rich have a certain responsibility for the poverty of everyone else.'

'Well, that's a case of guilt over living if ever I heard one. You know that there's nothing the rich can do to help the poor. If we all gave our money to the starving, there would be total economic depression and you'd end up with twice as many poor people as you started with.'

'That's not necessarily true.'

'Well, it certainly would do little to help. All that would happen would be that no one, instead of a few, would be able to lead the full, humanistic existence that you say is the object of life.'

'Yes. It's the object of life for everyone.'

'And if it isn't possible for all, isn't it better that some should do it rather than none at all?'

'I don't know. But what I do know is that the life led by your friends—gambling, racing and sitting in the sun doing damn all—that's not the full life.'

'Then what is?'

'I don't know. The pursuit of beauty or knowledge.'

'Being a don at Oxford, do you mean?'

'No, not that.'

'Well, what then? We can't all be artists and intellectuals

and write articles on the poor.'

Dawson saw it as a sign of the maturity of their relationship that they could argue like this. And there were other signs of this maturity. Each knew what irritated the other: Dawson sacrificed bacon for breakfast because Jenny hated the smell. Jenny took care not to crumple or disrupt the evening paper before Dawson came in in the evening. And, to get down to what is, after all, the basis of a relationship of this kind, their sexual exchanges had also matured. Jenny no longer had to be patient with the inhibitions of the former celibate, and Dawson now knew his rights and obligations. They would make love as normally as they would take a walk along the Embankment, though Dawson noticed that they did so less frequently than in the first months—and that they went out more often. But this, he knew, from the advice he had given to so many perplexed penitents, was a most essential part of the maturing process of a relationship. Moreover London was a city of many distractions which were tiring and hard to resist.

At one of these debilitating diversions, a charity ball, Dawson came across Theresa Carter once again. They were all in fancy dress as characters from Shakespeare's plays. Jenny who was dressed as Titania from *A Midsummer Night's Dream* had persuaded Dawson to go as Friar Lawrence from *Romeo and Juliet*. He wore a brown robe with a cowl, in the style of the Franciscan Order, with a rope around his waist and sandals on his feet. The costume caused some amusement because many of us there knew about Dawson and his past.

The ball was given in a large house about twenty miles from the centre of London—an eighteenth-century edifice now in the hands of the National Trust. During the day it was open to the general public who would pay five shillings to see the architectural and artistic beauties and wonder at the style of life of the former aristocracy. At night it was normally closed, inhabited by one or two watchmen who made their tea in the cellars and emerged only to see that no tapestry had been stolen or pipe had burst. Every now and then, however, when the worthiness of a particular cause seemed ripe, the house would be opened to relive its gracious past at a charge of twenty guineas for each couple that saw itself in the role. I cannot quite remember what particular disaster brought about that party. Perhaps it was at this time that Skopje was reduced to rubble, or was it Fréjus? Or it may have been massacre and famine in the Congo. I should know because our photographers must have been out there snapping the rotting sores and distended bellies. It does not really matter, but it was certainly something non-political and something special: it could not have been for the victims of Vietnam or the everyday misery of most of the world's inhabitants.

The spectacle was impressive. Imagine waiters in doublets serving wine from earthenware jugs, trestle tables loaded with sucking-pig and caviar, pewter plates piled with strawberries and melon, and thousands of men and women in Elizabethan costume. There were among them most of the kings of England from Henry IV to Henry VIII, including a variety of Richard IIIs. There were four Macbeths but only three Lady Macbeths, a number of Hamlets, Harry Hotspurs and two Falstaffs.

Dawson, the Friar, and Jenny Stanten, Titania, went in a party with Henry Poll as Julius Caesar and Benji as Polonius. Susan Poll was one of the Lady Macbeths. They spent the first part of the evening milling around with everyone else, greeting their friends and acquaintances or assessing the avenues for the evening's intrigue.

Towards midnight the party decided to eat the dinner that was represented by a detachable portion of their tickets. They went up the elegant staircase to one of the smaller rooms that were being used to feed the guests. Benji went off to find

Susan Poll who was missing, and returned not only with her but with a woman called Sylvia Lippert whom they all knew. She was dull and divorced from an American and it did not become clear why she had been asked to join them until Susan Poll came in with Sylvia's son, a twenty-two-year-old youth dressed as Macduff. This boy seemed to suffer from a dislike of his mother which he demonstrated, as well as the usual restlessness of his age. His eyes shone with contempt for those around him and, quite naturally, with lust for the prettiest woman present. He had thought that it might be Susan Poll, and so had Susan Poll, until they came into the dining-room when he saw Jenny and shifted his smouldering attention on to her.

The table was round and was set for eight. The seven of them sat down and a waiter removed the eighth place. The seating was arranged in what they all insisted was the only way in which husbands and wives, mothers and sons, could be separated. Dawson had Sylvia to his right and Susan Poll to his left. Next to her was Benji and next to him, Sylvia's son, Marshall. Jenny sat on the other side of this boy and Henry Poll between her and Sylvia. The table was too large for conversation between those opposite each other: they were limited, there, to those adjacent.

Dawson, for whatever reason, was tired and bored: but even if his mood had been different, he would not have affected the sulkiness of Susan Poll or the steady monologue of Sylvia Lippert. She directed it, anyway, as much to her right as to her left, and Henry Poll seemed more attentive. Only Jenny and Sylvia's son seemed to have any kind of conversation. Benji's attempts to join in seemed to fail, and so he turned to Susan Poll which did not improve her bad humour but left Dawson free to say nothing.

The food, though authentic, was overcooked and cool. Nor was the wine, disguised in its earthenware jugs, of a good vintage. It could have been anything. Dawson had hoped that there would be relief from the noise from below but the loud voices of Benji, Sylvia and Henry Poll made up for it.

'Who do you think is the most bored?' Susan Poll asked him.

'I don't know. Are you bored?'

'Of course I am. And so are you.'

'An expensive way to be bored,' said Benji.

'It's all the fault of you men who aren't interested in intelligent conversation. You're just after the prettiest and stupidest women.'

'You say that because you're so clever, darling,' said Benji.

'I know I'm clever; and I'm pretty too, but not pretty enough.'

'Not at all,' said Dawson abstractly.

'You couldn't tell the truth if you wanted to,' said the clever and plain Susan Poll.

'I'll tell the truth,' said Benji. 'After all, I'm disinterested.'

'Well then?'

'You're the cleverest woman in the room.'

'There. And the least attractive.'

'Susan, dear, I'm just as upset as you are. I'm sure I'm the funniest person here, but I'm a little too heavy and soft and I'm the wrong sex . . .'

They both had their eyes on Sylvia's son who at that moment rose from his chair. Jenny stood too.

'We're going to dance a minuet,' she said with a look from under her brows at Dawson.

The strawberries remained on their plates. Dawson finished his and then turned away from Susan Poll to listen to Sylvia.

'It's so difficult to know where to live these days, don't you know. I used to spend the autumn in New York, but now you can't walk down Fifth Avenue without being mugged as they call it. It'll soon be the same in London. And already the climate's so awful here and the taxes are so high that it's a wonder anyone stays. It's the people, of course. Malcolm liked Bermuda, but the people there are such bores. And it'd be the same in Spain or Italy or somewhere like that. Plenty of sun and swimming, but bores, bores wherever you go. No theatre. You've got the theatre here, but then there are the taxes. It really is awfully difficult to make up one's mind.'

Those who wanted were served with more strawberries. Then these plates were removed and the waiters brought coffee. Jenny's chair and the one next to it remained empty. Elizabethan goblets were then given to each man and they were offered a choice of port or brandy. Dawson took brandy. The women were offered liqueurs.

'Good heavens, Edward, that looks good,' Henry Poll shouted from the other side of Sylvia Lippert.

'What's that?' Dawson asked.

'You're imbibing holy wine, if I'm not mistaken. Saying a mass on the side.'

'Only unholy brandy, I'm afraid,' said Dawson.

The rest of the table stopped their conversations to listen to this exchange.

'Why don't you? Yes. Go on, say a mass,' said Benji.

'Yes, go on,' said Henry Poll.

'A black mass or a white one?' asked Dawson with a laugh.

'A black one sounds more fun,' said Benji.

Henry Poll flicked his fingers in the air. 'Hey, waiter, any bread there? Bring back the bread.'

'Unleavened, if you have it,' said Benji.

'Are you really going to?' asked Susan Poll.

'Just give us the *hocus pocus*,' said Henry Poll, 'unless of course you'd rather not.'

'If it amuses you,' said Dawson.

'Oh yes,' said Sylvia, 'and then you must hear my confession.'

Dawson looked at the two empty chairs and then at the door of the dining-room. A waiter came in with two rolls on one of the pewter plates. Henry Poll leaned across the table and filled his goblet with brandy. There was a silence. They waited.

'But I have to have the accoutrements,' said Dawson. 'I can't do it without the accoutrements.'

'Anything, old boy,' said Henry Poll. 'What else do you need?'

'For a Black Mass . . . I don't know . . . a naked woman, for a start.'

'Really,' said Benji. 'Does it have to be a woman?'

'If not a virgin,' said Dawson.

'That's unreasonable,' said Henry. 'But what about Sue?'

'Go to hell,' said Susan Poll.

'Here, Jenny,' said Henry Poll, as Jenny came back into the room, 'Edward's going to say a black mass.'

'Are you?' she asked. She was chewing her lip and looked angry.

'Impossible,' said Dawson. 'You need a naked woman.'

'And then you'd do it?'

'No. It's a joke.'

'Would it upset you?'

'Of course not.'

'Then why not play the joke?'

'Yes, go on,' said Henry Poll.

'You must,' said Sylvia.

'You can't disappoint us now,' said Benji.

'I tell you,' said Dawson, 'there has to be a naked woman.'

The frown concentrated further on Jenny's brow. 'If that's all you need,' she said, 'you can have me.' She then stretched her hands around to the small of her back to undo the clasp that held together the bodice of her costume.

'For God's sake,' Dawson said to her.

'Would you undo this?' she asked Sylvia's son, who stood behind her. With a look of curiosity on his face, he did so. Jenny herself took the other hooks from their eyes and the dress fell to the floor.

'Don't, Jenny,' Dawson said.

'Go on old girl,' said Henry Poll.

Jenny looked at neither of them but removed her slip with swift and deliberate gestures. The two waiters in the room looked nervously towards the door, but then returned to the fascinating display, for Jenny was now removing the remainder of her underclothes, uncovering her angular shoulders, broad back and small breasts with their disproportionately large nipples.

'Bravo,' said Benji.

'Good old Jenny,' said Henry Poll.

Dawson said nothing.

There were candles and flowers already on the table but Benji and Henry Poll now arranged them as decoration for an altar. Hands cleared it of plates and glasses. Jenny was then naked. 'Pray, Father, on my back or my front?' she asked, looking at Dawson in the face for the first time since she had returned to the room.

'On your back,' said Sylvia, 'it's always on your back, at least I think so.' And this was what Jenny did. She lifted herself on to the table and lay down on her back. Benji and Henry Poll, like two sub-deacons, brought the goblet and one of the two rolls in front of Dawson. And Dawson began: 'He, on the day before he suffered death, took bread into . . .' But here he stopped. He felt suddenly sick and involuntarily he vomited, a trickle of half-digested brandy, coffee, strawberries, sucking-pig and consommé-en-gelée dripping from his mouth on to the table-cloth and on to the stomach of his naked mistress, collecting in part in her navel.

'Shit,' she said, lifting herself up.

'I'm sorry,' he said. 'I just feel sick.'

He then left the room and went down the stairs to the cloakroom where he spewed the rest of the period dinner into the more contemporary lavatory. When he felt that his stomach was empty, he stood up. His eyes were wet and bloodshot. He could see this in the mirror. He also noticed that there were streaks of vomit down the front of his friar's habit. He took some paper and wiped it off, then leant over the basin and splashed water on to it, then dried the area with a towel.

He came out of the cloakroom. Benji was standing there. 'You all right?' he asked.

'Yes,' said Dawson. 'Where's Jenny?'

'She's tidying up,' he said. Then he went into the cloakroom.

Dawson walked to the door of the house and stood on top of the steps, thinking of nothing, concentrating on the sensation of the cold air on his skin—numb with alcohol. A girl and a boy passed him on their way out.

'Hello,' said the girl—a rich tone of voice.

'Hello,' he said.

'Don't you know who I am?' she asked.

'No,' he said.

'Ophelia,' she said, laughing. 'I recognized you in your habit.'

'Theresa,' he said.

'That's right,' she said and hesitated, but then followed the boy who had already gone down the steps on to the gravel.

Jenny came up beside him, her face and hair and clothes adjusted. 'Let's go,' she said.

'Yes.'

They drove back to London in the Italian car she had given Dawson as a birthday present two weeks before.

'Shit,' she said.

'What?'

'I thought I'd got over it.'

(Silence.)

'I mean I used to do things like that before I met you.'

'We were all drunk.'

'I'm sorry.'

'It doesn't matter.'

'No. You didn't mind? I mean . . .'

'They're just words, aren't they? It must have been that tepid sucking-pig.'

'Yes. No one would have eaten it if it had been called pork.'

They were silent between Hatfield and Hendon. Then Jenny said, 'It was that damned boy.'

'What about him?'

'Oh, he was so bloody. The conceit of boys of that age.'

'What sort of conceit?'

'Oh, you know: his generation aren't going to make the same mistakes as ours. That sort of thing.'

'He can't be so much younger than you are.'

'Six years.'

'That's not a generation.'

'No. But I wanted to shock him.'

'I should think you succeeded.'

'I hope so.'

(Silence.)

'And I was so fucking, bloody bored.'

Chapter Eleven

In September of that year Dawson's sister Sally passed through London with her family on the way to Southampton. Her husband had decided to accept the post he had been offered in Minnesota. They stayed for two nights with Jenny and Edward in the house in Cheyne Row.

'You've done very nicely for yourself,' Arnie said to Dawson as soon as they were alone.

'Yes, it's a nice place.'

'A house like this would cost twenty or thirty thousand pounds, these days.'

'Possibly.'

'A fat chance I'd ever have of making that kind of money.'

'Some people do.'

'Not at anything honest. It's all either inherited or made in some swindle. It's this sort of thing that's sickened me with England.'

They were walking to a pub—the sun on the painted houses, the light and the city dust.

Arnie never looked at anyone he spoke to. 'It's rotten, this country,' he went on, 'it's rotten all the way down with snobbery and class prejudice. You're all right, because you went to the right sort of school. That's why you get a woman like that Jenny of yours.'

'I'd have been quite happy if Jenny wasn't rich.'

'That's what you all say, but I can tell you that your Jenny would no more entertain the idea of a man like me with my accent and all that than she would a nigger or a Jew.'

'Less,' said Dawson.

'Well, I'm glad you admit it. Though how you can live with a woman as prejudiced as that, I don't know.'

'I've got to make use of what I've got.'

'You're quite right, you have. You stay and enjoy it. The first mate certainly deserves to go down with the sinking ship. But me, I'm getting out.'

They reached the pub and went into the saloon bar.

Jenny must have known that Dawson had a sister, and she must have been curious to see this relative, her husband and child. Perhaps she imagined one of those pleasant girl's friendships—the long and quick chat about children and men and homes. But when they did arrive to stay in her house for two days, Jenny was aghast. Prepared for a girl different to her brother in appearance and behaviour, she had not expected a woman different in social class. Though she dared to stick out her tongue at Arnie when his back was turned—and Dawson smiled—there was no tangible ground for disliking the blood relative. Her clothes were neat and clean: only their style was foreign—not foreign in the sense that they came from Paris or Rome, but rather the opposite, that they came from Leeds.

Jenny had told Dawson that she would give a dinner party for his sister and brother-in-law on the night before they left. They had decided to ask the usual lot of friends—Benji, the Polls and Sylvia Lippert, who now seemed to be included in their circle. Dawson assumed that the guests had all been invited but when the day came, Jenny said that the Polls could not come after all and neither could Benji. 'Anyway,' Jenny said, 'I don't think Arnie and Sally would like them.'

'Perhaps not: but we have to have someone.'

'Sylvia's coming, and she's bringing Marshall and her new friend.'

'And who else?'

'I asked Theresa Carter.'

'Why on earth did you ask her?'

'I thought you might like me to.'

'Of course not. What made you think that?'

'You were talking to her at that party.'

'We just said hello to each other as we were leaving.'

'Was that all? I thought you might like to get to know her on a new footing, if you see what I mean.'

'Well I don't.'

'It's too late now, I'm afraid. Anyway, I think she and Sally will get on quite well together, don't you?'

They sat at the round table in the kitchen, lit by candles. Jenny bent over the oven and lifted out a large bowl of rice with skewered beef and onions lying on the top. Dawson uncorked two bottles of red wine. Arnie sat straight in his chair and was caught by Sylvia's usual monologue. Sylvia's new lover, the publisher of Dawson's first visit to Jenny's house, asked Sally interested questions about the provinces. Sylvia's son sat silently next to the chair that was to be filled by Jenny. Dawson, holding, the wine, studied the back of Theresa's head. Her hair was brown. She leant her head back and he saw her neck—thinner than he had remembered it. Her legs, which he had glanced at as she came into the house, were not as good as Jenny's. He sat down next to her.

'How's your mother?' he asked.

Her cheeks seemed wider; the skin on her face was now clear and unblemished. . . .

'She's gone to Italy.'

Her voice was quieter, her eyes more quizzical.

'What are you doing?'

'Oh, nothing, really. I work in a gallery. You know . . .'

'What happened to the house?'

'Mum sold it. I've got a flat in Notting Hill.'

'Do you like living there?'

'Yes. It's nice—varied, you know, and there's a direct line to work.'

'The Central?'

'That's right.' She smiled. 'How've you been?' she asked.

'How do I look?'

'Oh fine,' she said, looking not at him but around the table.

'We're all a bit older,' he said.

She glanced back at him. 'Yes, you look older. When you were a priest, you had a rather wide-eyed look.'

'I'm glad I've lost that.'

'You shouldn't be. It was very attractive.' She smiled again.

The publisher was continuing to inform himself of the *mores* of the provinces. 'Are the morals the same in Leeds as they are in London?'

'What sort of morals?' Sally asked.

'When people say morals like that,' Dawson said to his sister, 'they mean sexual morals. Isn't that right?'

'Well, yes,' said the publisher. 'What other kinds are there?'

'There's said to be some wife-swapping in the North Riding,' said Sally. 'but I don't know about that. You read it in the papers, that's all.'

'It's always different in a capital city,' Jenny said, taking her place at the table.

'I'd imagined a lot of Madame Bovary's, to say the least,' said the publisher.

'You'll more likely find promiscuity among the younger girls,' said Dawson.

'Then it's high time I paid a visit to Nottingham. The prettiest girls in England are supposed to be in Nottingham.'

'Don't believe it,' said Sylvia. 'It's what they say about Des Moines, Iowa. If any girl in a town like that looks half-way decent, she goes to New York.'

'Is Iowa near to Minnesota?' Sally asked.

'Oh God, don't ask me,' said Sylvia.

'They're next to each other,' said Dawson.

'It's not the same in America, though,' said Arnie. 'The provinces there really have a life of their own. In fact they say that people are leaving New York and places like that because of the air pollution and the crime and that kind of thing.'

'Don't they have that in Minnesota?' asked Sally.

'No. Not where we're going. It's the best of America there: vigorous, competitive, rich, ready to put money into research and pay good men for good work. . . .'

Then Marshall Lippert spoke, his eyes fixed on Arnie, then his mother, then Dawson and finally Jenny. 'You wait and see,' he said. 'America is the trash-can of the world, our precious free-enterprise system has caused more suffering . . . ten million people don't have enough to eat and the Indians die on their reservations and everyone hates each other—the young hate the old, the blacks hate the whites . . .'

'Marshall was at Berkeley,' said Sylvia, 'you know . . . in California.'

'People can't talk to each other unless they're half drunk on gin or whisky,' her son went on, 'and as many people die of overeating as of starvation.'

'That's as may be,' said Arnie, 'but technically and scientifically and in management, they lead the world. '

'What use is there in running business if you can't run your own society?'

'Who can, these days?' the publisher asked.

'There are those who do,' said Sylvia's son. 'In China and Cuba . . .'

Early the next morning Dawson drove his sister, her husband and the child down to Southampton in the Lancia. Jamie was restless and the attention of the adults was distracted by his fidgeting.

'It was nice of Jenny to have had that dinner for us,' Sally said.

'Oh, it wasn't much trouble,' Dawson said with a wave of his hand.

'I expect she entertains a lot, does she?' Arnie asked.

'Yes, quite a lot.'

'I know, but she does it all herself,' said Sally. 'I think she's marvellous.'

'She has some help.'

'I know. But she cooks so well. Those simple things. She's wonderful.' Then she added. 'I'm glad you've got her, Eddie. You deserve a break.'

'Yes,' said Arnie, 'you can count yourself lucky.'

'Yes,' said Dawson. 'It is lucky to love someone and to be able to be with her.'

At the port Arnie went to see that the baggage, which had been sent by train, had arrived. Jamie left his mother and ran up and down the large hall of the Cunard terminal.

'It's sad to be going,' Sally said.

'There wasn't much to stay for, was there?' Dawson asked.

'I don't know. It was home.'

'Will you miss Mum?'

'Not really.'

'What, then?'

'I don't know. I bet they only have tea bags over there. No proper tea. You know.'

'They drink coffee.'

'I hate coffee.'

'You'll get used to it: and you'll meet new friends.'

'I'll miss you, Eddie. And I was just getting to like you . . . you're my brother, after all.'

'I'll come and see you over there.'

'Will you? I hope you do, but I won't count on it. The Atlantic's a bit like the grave, isn't it? You don't really, know if you'll meet up with anyone on the other side.'

Dawson now drove from Southampton to Oxford where he intended to collect the necessary information for his final article. It was to be on the subject of strikes, which were frequent in England at this time and stimulated continuous indignation in the general public. Dawson, a member of this public, was baffled by the stupidity and selfishness of these few men who would jeopardize and often damage the interests of the country just to gain some limited advantages for themselves.

Oxford was a centre of the British motor industry and there was at the time an unofficial strike at Karmer's engineering works which demonstrated in its classic absurdity the disruption to a nation's productivity that could be caused by a few men. Karmer's made the piston rings for a number of different models of cars and lorries; the rate and pace of their manufacture was geared most precisely to the production lines of several different factories so that the rings should be there when they were needed but would not pile up on the factory floor.

In summer the factory had closed down for the two week holiday. When the men returned from Blackpool, Brighton and the Costa del Sol, they found that their canteen had been repainted green. Now the committee of shop stewards had, before the holiday, specifically requested that this canteen be repainted yellow—the men had voted on it. The management had received the recommendation but they had not acted on it. The canteen was repainted in the colour it had been before.

The workers on the floor were so angry that they voted to strike. The union officials did their best to persuade them to go back to work, arguing that this was a small issue: but the men insisted that before they did so, they must see yellow paint over the green. The union then turned to the management, arguing that a new coat of paint, yellow over the green, would cost them less than half a day of the strike. But the management was now under the direction of the parent company in Pittsburg which thought an example must be made out of this issue if British workers were ever to learn American methods of industrial relations. The cost of the strike, though large, would quickly be made up by the automated and sophisticated routines they intended to install once the cussedness of the factory hands had been broken.

The leader of the strikers who emerged from the tame ranks of the regular union bureaucracy was a young shop steward called Mike McKeon. He had come to England from Belfast a few years before, and the newspapers quickly discovered that he had been dismissed from the shipyards there as an agitator. They also discovered that he was, or had been, a Communist.

The interest of the Press in this strike of less than eighty men was caused by its repercussions which had now reached the larger motor factories: for when their stocks of piston rings ran out, the production lines came to a halt. No alternative source seemed to exist: thus fifteen thousand fitters and painters and engineers were laid off. The half-finished saloons and trucks and sports cars destined for Paris and Atlanta, Rome and Bombay lay immobile in the unfamiliar silence of the factories.

Dawson was committed to the belief that all social phenomena have a scientific explanation and so a scientific solution. He was doubtful of simultaneous madness and saw no motive for mass crime. He felt sure that it must be ignorance that had led these men to act in this way—ignorance and misunderstanding. He arranged, therefore, to visit the leader of the strike, Mike McKeon, in his home in Oxford, to discover the nature of the ignorance and through his column, dissipate the misunderstanding.

He reached the city in the early afternoon. His appointment was not until six so he parked his car and walked out into the street, past the colleges and churches, down to the river. It was autumn, the beginning of the new term. The students and their girls walked past and beside him, giggling and careening, flapping their arms in excess of energy. Dawson walked on in these areas of the town, the areas of learning rather than of industry. It became quite dark. There were few people in the street. The groups left the pavements for parties or dances or dinners and Dawson was hungry, so he went to a cafe and ordered tea. There were other groups eating there, all young, all well-dressed, loud, unselfconscious, oblivious of the journalist, the strike—intent only on pure enjoyment, pure fun.

Dawson finished his bacon and eggs, paid his bill and went back to his car. He then drove across Magdalen bridge to Cowley. Here there were not the grimy, back-to-back slums he had expected, but fair-sized houses laid out in wide streets. He passed the gates of the various factories, numbered and guarded like the entrances to barracks or prisons. Scholarship, it seemed, was adorned—the object of men's vanity and sensibility: manufacture was not—the factories were huge and plain, existing only for their function, like the hangars at an airport.

Dawson found the street where McKeon lived and in the street he found the house. He parked his car and rang the bell. McKeon himself opened the door. He was thin, like Dawson, but smaller, with grey skin and brown hair; his eyes were bright blue.

'Come in,' he said, and Dawson bent his head to enter the house—a short corridor going to the stairs, the kitchen beyond the stairs, a front room, a back room and doubtless two bedrooms above.

'This is my wife,' McKeon said, introducing him to a small woman who came from the kitchen.

'I'll make some tea if you'd like some.' she said.

Dawson thought for a moment that he knew her—but it was only that she reminded him of Helen Sweet.

Mrs McKeon went back to the kitchen and her husband led Dawson into the front room, which faced on to the street, as in the house in Cheyne Row, but in a stricter sense: there would have been no privacy from every passer-by if the lower part of the windows had not been covered with muslin curtains. There was a fireplace of pale cream tiles, and a varnished dresser opposite. Between the two, taking the remaining space, were two armchairs and a sofa, all made of beige plastic. On one side of the fireplace there was a small table covered with books, letters and newspapers. On the other side there was a television.

'I've read some of your articles,' McKeon said. 'They're not bad.'

'But not good?'

'There's never anything in that kind of paper that I'd call good.'

'You must have very high standards.'

'Perhaps.'

'How do you judge an article?'

McKeon looked up at him. 'You're a journalist. How should I judge an article?'

'I don't know . . . its liveliness, I suppose, and the style.'

'What about the truth of it?'

'Yes. Accuracy, of course.'

'No. Truth.'

McKeon had an odd accent—part Irish, part Scottish—and from his mouth 'Truth' came out as a long word, almost like a low whistle.

'It's curious,' said Dawson. 'It seems old-fashioned to talk of truth in relation to newspaper work these days.'

'You can say that again.'

'It was misused, that's why. Objectivity and accuracy amount to the same thing.'

McKeon did not reply. His wife came in with a tray of tea. She put it down on the dresser and poured out a cup for Dawson and for her husband and then left them again.

'What do you want from me, anyway?' McKeon asked, shifting his weight on the sofa.

'I want your point of view.'

'But not objectivity and accuracy?'

'Well, yes, from your point of view.'

'And you'll get it from the other side?'

'Perhaps . . . I don't know.'

'And somewhere between their objectivity and my objectivity will lie your objectivity and that'll be the truth?'

'Not necessarily. It might be the same as yours or the same as theirs, in between or outside the whole framework of the issue. I'm interested in the phenomenon, not the incident.'

'Well, I'll give you both sides. Our side is that we use the canteen so we should decide the colour of its walls. They say that they own the factory and owe it to the shareholders to extract maximum profits. Yellow walls show the dirt more than green walls, therefore the walls must be green.'

'That's all it is?'

'On the surface.'

'And underneath?'

'Underneath? I don't advise you to go underneath, Mr Dawson. You'll get out of your depth and you'll drown.'

'You seem to have me sized up.'

'As I said, I've read your articles.'

'You could educate me. I'm ready to learn.'

McKeon wore flannel trousers and an open-necked check shirt. He had cloth slippers on his feet. 'They'd never let you print it if you learnt it.'

'They'll print what I write.'

'Well, I'll tell it, and I'll tell it from our point of view because I don't think there is any objectivity around. We don't like the system, the capitalist free-enterprise system, because it's not free in any way that means anything to us. The canteen—that's an issue, but it goes further and deeper into the whole structure of industrial relations—the structure where the responsibility of the management is to the shareholder, not to the worker on the floor nor even to the consumer, the public.

'Now you'll say that we've got our freedom and democracy because we get to vote every five years for a member of parliament, but that's not a kind of freedom and democracy that means anything to us. All the papers, the radio, the television talk as if there's no alternative to the way things are. Even your liberals—and I count you a liberal—they only want little reforms here and there. They don't want a radical change that would take power out of money and put it into the hands of human beings.

'Of course we've got certain civil liberties so we can organize and that: but we've not got the money and we've not got the time. The financial structure of newspapers in this country is such that they need advertising—and advertising only goes to the papers which support the *status quo*.

'Our servitude is very real, Mr Dawson. If you'd ever worked in a factory, you'd know about it. But the chains are difficult to see because they're in the mind—in the mind of the people who control what's said and heard or spoken all over the country—on television, in the schools, the universities—it's all the same.'

'Do you really believe that there's a plot?' Dawson asked. 'A conspiracy to exploit the workers, and all that?'

'I don't know,' said McKeon, 'I've never made up my mind on that. You don't need many to preserve the *status quo* because most people just go along. It's a matter of a small tap with a little stick to keep the ball rolling. But there are people who make sure that the ball gets its small tap and you could call that a conspiracy.'

'I don't believe that such a conspiracy exists among journalists.'

'You say they'll print what you write?'

'Of course.'

'Try writing what I've said.'

'I will, if you like. I'll give your point of view. It's what I came to find out.'

McKeon smiled at him. 'You were a monk, once, weren't you?'

'Yes.'

'I think there's still a little bit of that monastic simplicity about you. No offence, mind you . . .'

'Perhaps the Communist party puts you in blinkers?'

'Perhaps.'

'Wait until you read my article. I'll prove that there's no conspiracy.'

'No basic assumption of the *status quo*? No sneer at social-ism. No consensus?'

'None. The Party line. You'll see.'

'You'll realize what you're doing?'

'I think so.'

'They've nearly beaten us, you see. The men can't take much more: they all listen and read. They've got to. And their wives keep on at them. Every paper they look at—there they are, traitors, saboteurs and all that.'

'Perhaps that's what they are,' said Dawson. 'I don't know. Your employers probably believe in a conspiracy as much as you do. But I'll prove to you, anyway, that it's all in your imagination.'

Dawson left McKeon and went back to Oxford to the foyer of the Randolph Hotel. He sat down at once to write his article while McKeon's words remained in his memory. He had come to write on the cause of the strike, but now kept his word and wrote on its purpose.

Chapter Twelve

It had taken Dawson a very short time to write the article. For the first time he had known just what he wanted to say and how to say it. As he drove back to London that night he continued to write the article in his mind—ranging far beyond the issue of the Karmer strike to wider issues of social democracy. McKeon had set off a train of thought which went fast and far like a new hypothesis for a physicist. The first formula had been wrong; the second inadequate. Perhaps at last he had found the answer to the question he had asked throughout his life—how to help others: the truth, as McKeon had called it.

Was he, then, to become a Communist? There came from his memory images of Communism—Russia, Stalin, torture and totalitarianism—things his mother had told him, things he had been taught at school. But McKeon had not had the face of a torturer. . . . A kind of weariness came over Dawson. The enthusiasm passed, leaving a backwash of depression. Could he change again? Could he say, to Jenny and others, that he had found the answer for a third time? It would depend, he thought, on what happened to the article.

It was eight when he reached London. He drove straight to Fleet Street. He waited for ten minutes in the lobby of the paper and then was told that Allenby could see him. He went up to the assistant editor's office. 'I've finished the last article,' he said to Allenby. 'I thought I'd bring it in to see what you thought of it.'

'I'm glad you did, Eddie,' Allenby said. 'We can start talking about the next series.'

Dawson handed him the article and sat down in silence,

keeping his eyes on his clasped hands while Allenby read what he had written. The secretary came in with letters to be signed: Allenby asked her to bring some tea and then went back to the article.

'Yes,' he said when he had finished.

'What do you think?' asked Dawson.

'It's not very like the others, is it?'

'Is that a bad thing?'

'I don't know if it's a bad thing, exactly,' Allenby said. 'I think it's a little high-flown in places, if you see what I mean, but that isn't what's wrong with it. It's just that the general line . . . the theme. . . . I'd like Demuth to have a look at it.' He picked up his telephone and asked for Demuth. A few minutes later Demuth came in.

'Hello, Eddie,' he said.

'Can you sub this, Tom,' Allenby said, 'and then let us see what you've made of it.'

'All right,' Demuth said, taking Dawson's article and leaving them again.

'I had intended to give the striker's point of view,' Dawson said.

'I see. You don't really say that, do you?' said Allenby.

'No. It's my point of view as well.'

'Is it? I mean, do you really believe all that?'

'Yes, I think so.'

'You saw McKeon, didn't you?'

'Yes.'

'He's quite eloquent.'

'I suppose so. I don't know.'

'You see, Eddie, in a feature like this, people want to know what you think, not what McKeon thinks.'

'It is what I think.'

'Then you seem to have changed your mind on a lot of basic issues since last month.'

'Perhaps.'

'Which is confusing, don't you see?'

'Well, it might make the article more interesting. I mean, I've never read the strikers' point of view.'

'Perhaps not. But you're not a striker at Karmer's.'

'No.'

'You're expected to be a responsible journalist, to look on things from the larger point of view.'

'I think I do. I think that's what I said, isn't it, that the strikers' interest is really the long-term interest of the country?'

'You can't think that.'

'Why not?'

'Because it isn't.'

'Who says it isn't?'

'The consensus . . .'

'The consensus could be wrong.'

'And you could be wrong.'

'Yes.'

'As it stands it looks as if you're playing a sort of intellectual trick on our readers. Twisting things round to make it look as if the interests of a minority are really the interests of the majority. Casuistry, I'd call it.'

Dawson shrugged. 'I meant it. You've just got to accept it.'

Allenby's secretary came back into his office with two cups of tea in cardboard containers. 'You don't take sugar, do you, Mr Dawson,' she said. Dawson smiled and said no, he did not.

'You see, Edward,' Allenby went on, 'you haven't been in journalism for long. If you'd been in it as long as I have, you'd realize that our so-called freedom of the press is a tenuous thing. Newspapers with large circulations like ours have to be responsible if they are to retain respect: and if they lose respect, they'll soon lose freedom. The country can't afford this kind of speculative dissent on very crucial issues. It's like the war. Freedom was limited then: and even now we have the "D" notices—a sort of voluntary censorship.'

'Yes, I see that.'

'Now this question of the strike is very crucial because we're a trading nation. If we printed your article as it stands, it would give confidence not just to the people at Karmer's, but to the same sort of men all over the place. The country just couldn't afford that.'

'Do you mean you won't print it?'

'Not as it stands, no.'

'McKeon said you wouldn't.'

'It looks as if you were taken in by McKeon hook, line and sinker.'

'As you said, he's eloquent.'

'Will you re-write it?'

'I don't know if I could.'

Demuth came back into the office. Dawson looked up at him. 'I've broken the Party line, haven't I?' he said

Demuth did not smile. 'You just don't know all the tricks of the trade yet, Eddie.'

'Did you sub the article?' Allenby asked.

Demuth handed some other sheets of paper to Allenby, who looked through them, sipping the tea out of the cardboard cup. Then he handed the new pages of typescript to Dawson. 'See what you think of this.'

Dawson did not read far. His article was parodied. The meaning was changed, turned around to lambast the very line of thought he had tried to defend. Only his phrases and his style had been retained.

'What do you expect me to say?' he asked Allenby.

'It doesn't matter much.'

'No.'

'It's your last article. We'll print it anyway.'

'I'll withdraw it.'

'You can't. Read your contract. You sent it in and we subbed it, that's all.'

Dawson turned to Demuth. 'I didn't think you'd do a thing like that.'

'You're just not a professional, Eddie.'

'So I see.'

'It's a pity,' said Allenby. 'We'd hoped to get you to do a new series. The others all went down well.'

Dawson stood up to go.

'If I thought you really believed it,' said Allenby, 'it might be different. But I'm not having a Communist like McKeon using this paper through a sucker.'

To someone as good-natured and even-tempered as Dawson, anger was a rare emotion and, if righteous, a delicious one. He left Allenby and the paper, damning them in his mind, and drove back across London to Chelsea furious and exhilarated. Thank God there was Jenny, someone who would share his indignation and help the development of his new ideas. That was love, he thought—the foundation of one's personality and ideas, like the meeting of two pillars at the apex of an arch, a point that could bear any weight.

The house was empty. Dawson made himself a cheese sandwich and poured himself a whisky and soda. It was ten at night. He tried to read the evening paper but could not: his mind kept returning to the article, the strike, McKeon, Allenby and Demuth. What hypocrisy and treachery there was in those jovial journalists, howling all the time about the great British tradition of the freedom of the press. What a grotesque swindle of the people; what a cruel twisting of their minds to print only what was sound—and invent unimportant issues and run them like a Punch and Judy show. He wished Jenny was there, to agree or disagree.

At half past ten he went out on to the terrace. It was warm for September and he could hear a group of people talking in the garden of the house next door. He could hear them, but he could not make out what they were saying. He went back into the drawing-room and, as if to quieten his turbulent mind, he put on a record of Vivaldi, but that only seemed to irritate him and after a few bars he took it off. He could only think that Jenny had taken the children to a film or the circus. He poured himself another drink. At a quarter to eleven the telephone rang. He picked it up and listened.

'Eddie?'

'Jenny. Where are you?'

(Silence.)

'Hello,' he said. 'Jenny? Where are you? It's a bad line.'

'Oh darling,' he heard her say.

'Where?'

'I'm in Paris.'

'Paris? Why on earth . . .?'

(Pause.)

'I'm with Marshall.'

'Who?'

'Marshall, you know, Sylvia's son.'

'Why?'

'Oh Eddie . . .'

'I mean, are you with him . . . just him?'

'Yes.'

'I mean, are you in love with him?'

(Pause.)

'I don't know.'

'What are you doing . . . I mean, why are you in Paris?'

'We're not staying here.'

'When will you be back?'

'We're going on.'

'Where?'

'To Mexico.'

'To Mexico? Why, for God's sake?'

'Darling . . . you wouldn't understand.'

'Where are the children?'

'They're all right.'

'Where are they?'

'In Northamptonshire.'

'I see.'

(Silence.)

'Darling . . . I really didn't want to hurt you.'

'No. You've left me, have you?'

(Pause.)

'. . . oh dear.'

'No. It's all right.'

'I thought it was the best way. Just to go.'

'Yes.'

'Don't hate me.'

'No.'

'I'll ring again.'

'Yes.'

'Goodbye, darling, for now.'

'Goodbye.'

Dawson put the telephone on its receiver. He sat down and held his glass tightly in his hand, but the ice was not cold enough to burn. It only wetted the palm of his hand. He sat quite still.

Things were left like that. Dawson, alone in the house, the house no longer his home, the owner absent—absent in body, disengaged emotions, woman from man, property rights, residency implications. Outside: the noise—motors, motor horns, human voices. People with plans—lifelong, daylong, private or implicit in their employment. Appointments. Inside: quiet—the sound of the electric clock in the kitchen, the oil burner of the water-heating system stopping and starting automatically following the rise and fall of the temperature in the water tank. Oil in the tanks for the burner. Food for the man in the cupboards and the refrigerator. Electricity through cables from a central source for light after the setting of the sun.

The telephone rings. Dawson seizes it, expecting her soft voice.

'Mr Dawson.'

'Yes.'

'Mr Dawson, Mr Allenby would like to speak to you.'

'Yes.'

'Edward?'

'Yes.'

'Good morning. I'm sorry about the article. No hard feelings, I hope?'

'What?'

'The article. The Karmer's strike article.'

'Oh yes.'

'No hard feelings?'

'No.'

'Good. I was just calling to ask where Jenny was.'

'She's gone abroad.'

'Yes. So I heard. To South America, isn't it?'

'To Mexico.'

'Is it true that she's gone to join some guerrillas?'

'I don't know.'

'No, well, never mind.'

Dawson made himself something to eat—scrambled eggs and coffee, a meal like breakfast though it was now two in the afternoon. He left the plate and cup on the table when he had finished and went up to their bedroom, sitting for a time on the bed. Silence. The only sound came from the tap and the cistern. The faint sound of traffic.

He went up another flight of stairs into the children's room, then into the nurse's room. He looked through her drawers and examined the clothes she had left in them—neat piles of blue blouses and a white suspender belt in which the rubber had perished.

As he came down the stairs again he heard the door bell.

He went to the door and opened it. It was Theresa. 'May I come in?' she asked.

'Jenny isn't here,' he said.

'I know.'

Theresa walked past him and came into the panelled hallway. She unbuckled the belt of her macintosh.

'How did you know?' Dawson asked.

'She rang me.'

'What?'

'Yes. She just called, from Paris. They were at the airport.'

'I was waiting for her to call me.'

'Yes. She told me that. She said she couldn't. . . I don't know. She couldn't bring herself to, or something.'

For a time, now, neither of the two said anything. Theresa took off her macintosh and sat down at the kitchen table with an ease she would not have shown had Jenny been in the house. Dawson waited for a moment in the hall and then followed her into the kitchen.

'Can I make some coffee,' she asked.

'Yes,' he said. 'I think there is some.' And he went to the cupboard and took out the coffee tin with a kind of care and possessiveness. He knew the level of the coffee in that tin and valued it more than it might seem to merit.

Theresa treated the coffee with no such care. She put them into the machine and thrust the machine on to the stove. She then took the cup and plate off the table and washed them at the sink.

'What did she say?' Dawson asked.

'She just told me.'

'Was it warm there?'

'I didn't ask her.'

'Do you know Sylvia's son?'

'I met him . . . here.'

'Yes. I met him too, but I don't remember him.'

'He's not up to much.'

'What is it, then?'

'He's young, and good-looking, I suppose.'

'Do you think it's just that?'

'Yes.'

'Will she get bored with him?'

'Yes, perhaps. I don't know.'

They sat together at the table.

'You haven't shaved,' she said.

'No,' he said, looking at his chest and picking at his shirt. 'I didn't really sleep last night.'

'Perhaps you shouldn't be drinking coffee.'

'No. I'll have a drink in a minute. Tell me, why did she ring you?'

'She was worried.'

'Why didn't she ring me?'

'I should think she didn't dare.'

'Why not? I don't understand.'

'Perhaps she feels ashamed.'

'Why?'

'Well, for leaving you like that.'

The expression on Theresa's face, if Dawson had bothered to notice it, must have been a pure and classic example of feminine enigma. Certainly, she had come on a mission, but its nature was unclear and so the level of tautness and excitement was ambiguous. There was a touch of breathlessness in her speech and less modulation in the tone of her voice than was usual.

'She was always free to do that, to leave me,' Dawson said to her with a wave of his hand. 'We weren't married.'

'I know, but she knew it would hurt you.'

'Did she?'

'She knew you still loved her.'

'Yes.'

Theresa went out to buy some food for the evening. When she got back, Dawson had already drunk a lot. She said nothing but drank herself, quickly, whisky with ice. They got drunk together.

'Why did she ring you, I wonder?' he asked.

'I told you,' she said. 'She wanted me to see that you were all right.'

'Yes, but why you?'

'She said she tried Bobby Winterman but couldn't get hold of him.'

'And you're the only other person who's my friend, not hers.'

'Perhaps. I don't know.'

'It's very kind of you.'

'I don't mind.'

Theresa went down to the kitchen and grilled steak and made salad and rice. The steak was crisp and the rice soggy but Dawson did not notice. They hauled the television on to the kitchen table and watched until midnight, drinking all the time.

'She won't come back, will she?' he said.

'I don't know.'

'She never does.' He leant back, half asleep.

'Come on,' said Theresa. 'I'll get you to bed.'

Dawson allowed himself to be helped upstairs: he permitted Theresa to help him undress because he was too drunk to help himself. He fell asleep in his underclothes.

Theresa Carter had recovered from her disinclination to eat some time ago. This psychological syndrome had come over her soon after her father's death and had been attributed to it. Her mother had always suspected that it was due to something more—to Father Dawson, in fact—and had confided this to most of her acquaintances, including Jenny Stanten. The illness had reached a stage where a drip was contemplated in order to keep her alive: her heavy bones protruded from her body and her eyes were sunken into their sockets. But then she seemed to take hold of herself: she left her mother's house and moved into a flat of her own. She found a job and gradually gained weight. Over a period of six months her body had regained its previous proportions but the change that had taken place in her personality seemed more settled. She became known for her kindness, a quality somewhat out of fashion like good character and lace caps. She went out with boys as before, but whenever their conversation or behaviour suggested a certain kind of feeling or sequence of gestures, she withdrew: and to the most persistent she confided that she was in love or had been in love and really could not love anyone else at the moment. And with those who said that they did not want her love but that fucking was fun she replied that she was no longer fifteen years old and sex without love was nothing.

She kept up appearances. Her clothes were always clean, neat and strictly fashionable. She never got fat, and though her figure remained large her face took on a beauty quite different in kind to her previous prettiness. Her eyes lingered on the faces of those she was listening to, expressing the stillness of indecipherable thoughts. Instead of a bouncy grin she bestowed a smile which, like her eyes, suggested some understanding of something which one might describe with music but never with words.

One afternoon the children's nanny let herself into the house in Cheyne Row. 'I hope you don't mind, Mr Dawson,' she said, 'I didn't know whether you'd still be here or not.' She went to the top of the house to collect some of the children's clothes and some of her own. She must have noticed Theresa's nightgown on Henrietta's bed.

Every evening after she had finished work at the gallery, Theresa would come back to Cheyne Row. Sometimes she would go to her flat first to collect clean clothes or her letters: but always, by seven, she was with Dawson, preparing his food or drinking with him. He never asked her to come, and she never spoke of it. After dinner they would read or watch television or go to a film.

Ten days after Jenny had left him, Dawson met Theresa in the hall of the house as she came in.

'I must leave this house,' he said.

'Yes,' she said.

'It's a nuisance, though. All the business of . . .'

'You can stay with me, if you like.'

Dawson packed his things, his own clothes and books and records, into two suitcases and they moved over to Notting Hill in a taxi. He left the Lancia Flavia in the street in Chelsea, but he kept the key to the house.

Theresa's flat was mean when compared to the house in Cheyne Row—but for a capital city it could be considered an adequate habitation. It consisted of the top floor of an Edwardian house in Kensington Park Gardens. There was a large living room with arches at either end, a kitchen, a bathroom and a small bedroom that had as its view the garden that was shared by this row of houses and a similar row in the next street.

Theresa had no instinct for furnishing and decorating her flat. There were the signs of several attempts to make the living room more pleasant. Three of the walls were painted blue: the fourth, with the two windows, was covered with wallpaper of a geometric pattern. The chairs were mixed: one was an old armchair which Theresa had apparently re-covered herself, another a contemporary design of a year or two before. The sofa could be made into a bed and Dawson slept on it for a time. The floor was carpeted in grey but parts of this carpet were stained and parts worn.

In the same way the books on the shelves were the sort that were bought by Book Clubs—general classics or the commonly popular. Many of them were in paperback editions. In the bathroom there were empty hair-sprays on glass shelves caked with circles of dried toothpaste. Theresa was puncti-lious with her own appearance but had not bothered much about her flat. Of course she had not had a chance to prepare it for Dawson, nor had she been living there for ten days. Nevertheless, it was a girl's flat: there were no pictures on the wall but faded psychedelic posters and immense photographs of Marlon Brando and Humphrey Bogart. Some might have found this touching, but Dawson did not.

Chapter Thirteen

I saw more of Dawson now. We had lunch together at least once a week and it was during these sessions of self-revelation that I learnt of his life what I had not already known. He talked a good deal of Jenny and I tried to persuade him that he should be glad to be rid of her.

He needed some help in financial matters, since Theresa could not keep him in the way Jenny had done. I was able to arrange for a new series of feature articles. I was not sure how the emotional turbulence would affect his writing, but the deadline was far off and the subject matter of the series was left to him.

The confessions were not one-sided: he was interested in my relationship with a girl I had made up my mind to marry and would cross-question me on the nature of my love.

'Do you think it will last?' he asked.

'Yes, I think it will,' I said. 'You know . . . we've both been through a lot and we know what we're doing.'

'But what sort of commitment do you feel you are making in marrying her?'

'I don't know. We have the same ideas about things. We suit each other.'

'What, you mean, it's a sort of happy combination of companionship and sexual attraction?'

'Yes, but it's more than that. I suffer without her.'

'Yes, that's love. Suffering without her. But you don't suffer when you're with her?'

'Of course not.'

'That can happen, you know, with a certain kind of love.'

I smiled. 'I'd never marry someone if I suffered both when

she was there and when she wasn't there.'

'No. I'm sure you're right. Marriage is best based on a sort of heightened friendship.'

In early December news reached us of what had become of Jenny Stanten and Marshall Lippert. A freelance journalist sent in the story from Caracas. The English woman and the American youth had arrived there from Mexico City with addresses and recommendations from radical student leaders in the United States. These contacts found some difficulty in understanding what the two 'Anglos' wanted, since neither could speak Spanish, but when they were shown the rifles they had concealed in their hide suitcases they understood. Brothers in fantasy, they guided the two inland to a be-leaguered *fuoco* of fifteen guerrillas.

They were not alone in their fantasy. The Venezuelan police too, if not the American Secret Service, believed in plots and revolutions. Whether they had read about Mrs Stanten's departure in the English newspapers, or whether they were simply suspicious of tourists travelling in areas where there is nothing to see, is not known: but like the journalist, they follow the trail of the young man in blue jeans and the lady in divided skirts and bush jacket. The evening after they had joined the guerrillas, the camp was ambushed by the police. Three of the guerrillas were killed—a Cuban, a French sympathizer and an Argentinian dentist. Nine escaped into the jungle. The rest were arrested and these included the two new recruits. They were taken back to Caracas where Marshall Lippert was incarcerated. Jenny, it seems, had come to some kind of understanding with the colonel who had captured her and was only under house arrest in the Venezuelan capital.

It was impossible to keep this story out of the paper and we had a scoop on it, but I did manage to tell Dawson before it broke. He listened and took it in and said nothing.

In January I was married to Arabella Cooper and it was more than six weeks before I saw Dawson again. When I did, he told me that he too had decided to get married, to Theresa. He wondered if Arabella and I would be witnesses at their wedding. I asked him, obliquely, why it was that he was getting married. 'Oh, I don't know,' he said. 'We both just rather wanted to get married.'

And the wedding took place, in a registry office, with myself and my wife the only others present. Then they went back to living as before.

From the moment they married their relationship deteriorated as if their feelings could not bear the weight of the formal institution. I blame myself now for not knowing then, and so not warning Dawson, that companionship is not necessarily enough. Sex is an unpredictable element in our lives and any erotic sentiment can turn sour: but with those two it can never have existed. It may have been that Theresa did not react as a woman should react and enjoy and complete the process of coition. There was something phlegmatic in her nature which may have been strongly expressed in her behaviour in this respect. Dawson, after all, was not used to ladylike composure on the bridal bed.

Thus they made love infrequently and when they did it was, as often as not, when they were drunk. Dawson, on his own admission, thought wistfully of other women, though he never said whether he still thought of Jenny Stanten. He took to working late at night and Theresa became injured and perplexed. She worried that they did not make love, and did her best to tempt him—not from enthusiasm, but just to do what she felt should be done. At night she powdered and scented her body—she hoped it might excite him—but her nightdress was made of cheap nylon and he was used to the most intricate lace. Her preparations had no effect: nor did the inadvertent touch of her leg or sight of her body.

Every afternoon and every night, Dawson sat at his desk in Theresa's flat, but each time he tried to put his pen to the paper and write, his mind faltered. He was now conscious of the complexity of truth. To write a journalistic essay was no longer a simple matter of observation and judgement. There were other people's points of view—the readers' prejudices and the editors' concept of their responsibility. Moreover, there were the rights of the human beings he might write about—the tramp's idea of himself, the drunk's idea of himself. These imagined pressures and opinions came down on each thought as it began to take shape. He felt himself a pig-in-the-middle with no point of view of his own.

'It's Saturday, Edward,' Theresa said to him. 'Let's go for a walk or something.'

'I can't possibly. I must work.'

Theresa spent her week-ends reading novels and newspapers, shopping and cooking those meals with little taste. They would eat them largely in silence, Dawson glancing at a book or a magazine but retaining enough self-respect not to read them at table. Theresa did her best to talk to him.

'Don't you think,' she once asked, 'that the Church is right, really, to make marriage a binding institution?'

'No. Why?'

'Well, it is a practical business, isn't it, and not so romantic?'

'That's true to the extent that priests can't conceive of love, so they can't write it into Canon Law.'

On another occasion: 'One sees the point of birth control, sometimes, don't you think? I mean, the Church being so strict about it. Why does one ever have children if it isn't sort of accidental?'

'It's quite possible to make up one's mind on practical grounds. We couldn't have one, for example, because you have to go on working until we know how much I can make as a free-lance journalist: and there isn't room in the flat.'

'I get three hundred a year from my shares.'

'That isn't enough to make any difference.'

A third occasion. 'I wish I did believe in God,' Theresa said. 'I was much happier when I did.'

'Of course,' said Dawson in his normal irritated tone of voice. 'They were the happiest days of our life: but it's a childish illusion all the same.'

'Are you just as sure as ever?'

'Of course I am. More so. I've become averse to Christians. There's something soft and unpleasant about them.'

Dawson struggled to write, to communicate to other human beings the truth that was represented in his own being and consciousness. He laboured at his desk to peel away the layers of self-deception and to know himself. What was he? What did he live for? Was there an aim, a theme or an inspiration in his life? He would sit for hours at a time turning his pen between his fingers, writing ideas on scraps of paper but not proceeding with them. What did he love? What did others love? Was he unique, or was he like other men? His wife was dull, like theirs: and like them he lived under incessant financial insecurity. His work was different, but like anyone else, he had to compromise his own principles, his own standards. But others seemed to have simple consolations for the dreariness of their life, such as an enthusiasm for football. Was it that that kept them alive? Saturdays at the stadium? August on the beach

In himself he was sure that there must be some single principle which would give shape to his life. He had had it in Catholicism and he had had it when he had rejected religion: he thought he had had it from McKeon, but now, somehow, he had lost it. It seemed that everyone else must have it but him, for what else kept them alive? Or could it be that most men lived in a despair so slothful that obedience to instinct was all that led them to survive?

Days of cogitation did not reveal that one principle of under-standing which would unify all his values and convictions. He was still lost within himself, unable to write a word. It occurred to him that this knowledge had eluded him because it had slipped from his consciousness into his subconscious: so he attempted to clear his mind of conscious thoughts and hope that this space would allow the submerged wisdom to come to the surface where it would be comprehended. He sat, empty-headed, and waited: but the only speck of awareness was the feeling of taut nerves in his stomach. The first con-scious thought which involuntarily emerged was an impulse to take a knife and sever this strain, lacerating the tight liga-ments, swamping the tension in blood.

Was this how his father had died? This thought, this memory, may also have come from his subconscious. Perhaps he had discovered the reason for his father's suicide—the knowledge that life is painful, without meaning and best brought to an end. Was this truth? That a knife should be taken in the hand to sever those intestines which send one running three times a day to cram the mouth with starch and grease and wash them down with hot and tepid liquids?

Theresa returned in the evening and they sat together in silence. Alcohol served no purpose. Television was nothing but a flickering light. Dawson's eyes never met hers, but occasionally they lolled on to her stolid calves and the un-loved features of her face.

'What have you been doing?' she asked.

'Thinking.'

'What about?'

'My father. Why he killed himself.'

'I wonder,' she said. 'I mean, do you think it's acceptable to kill yourself, if you aren't, well, getting much out of life or putting much into it?'

'If life is more pain than pleasure, it's an obvious thing to do. You just have to overcome the instincts which force you to stay alive.'

And, with enthusiasm, the next day, after breakfast, he came to see this struggle with nature as a majestic task—a hallowing of spirit and will. The meaning to his life would be the ending of it.

He knew that it must be gradual—a matter of weeks. He would not now cut his wrists or jump from the window because he was not frenzied or demented but calm. His suicide would be just as he imagined his father's to have been: not a mental aberration, but a philosophical statement.

He went to the kitchen and returned to his desk with a box of matches. He struck one and held it under his fingers. Pain. But why not? He kept his one hand, holding the match, under the fingers of the other. He forced pain upon himself to demonstrate that his will was outside his body's coating of nerves, and could prove its superiority over instinct and reflex action.

He assumed, of course, that he should document his demise —not as a shoddy article for a daily paper, but as a scientific and spiritual treatise. And he wrote, with his unharmed right hand, about the suppression of rebellion in the nerves of the left. He plotted, too, the course to his ultimate death. Days of fasting—the conquest of hunger. Night without sleep—the defeat of fatigue. The complete eradication of all sexual urges and reactions. When, finally, he took his own life, it would be as a calm stroll into the fiery furnace.

Theresa returned again as usual, which interrupted and annoyed her husband. He stayed at his desk and declined a cocktail with a wave of his hand. How gross the animality of women seemed when a man was groping with his destiny. Secretly, within his skull, he plotted as to how he might hide his fasts and vigils from Theresa, for he had no wish to admit her to the laboratory of his mind. He was afraid that she might have sensed what he was up to, since she looked inwardly perplexed: but she spoke cheerfully to him, even though he rarely answered her.

'Mary—you know, the other girl at the gallery—she's definite about being pregnant now and she says she's quite pleased. She says she'd like a baby even if she isn't married, because she might never get married and never have one. I wonder. I think she'll just use it to get her friend to leave his wife. I'm sure that's what she's after, don't you think so?'

She cooked an omelette and baked potatoes and made a salad with weak dressing. Dawson came to the table and ate, joylessly, angry even at satisfying his appetite against his will. Theresa looked at him and pursed her lips: Dawson looked at his food, then away, and said nothing.

'It's awful, a situation like that. Mary's, I mean. There are the three of them and someone's got to suffer. She says she really wishes his wife would die. He probably wants her to as well.'

She cleared away the plates.

Dawson moved to the sofa and sat there drinking coffee. Theresa washed the dishes and then came and sat near him. He took up a weekly review and read it, without much interest—but it preserved his solitude. She took picked up a magazine and did not read it.

'I wonder if there's anything on television,' she said and leant forward to switch on the set. Dawson gave an irritated grunt, so she went back to her magazine. He felt her eyes on him but he never met them to see their expression.

At half past nine, Theresa stood up and said that she was going to bed. Dawson, of course, was delighted because it meant he could try a night without sleep. He even returned the kiss she bent over to lay on his cheek. She left the living room. He heard her in the bathroom—running the bath, pissing, washing, splashing, brushing her teeth, rinsing her mouth, drinking, swallowing. Then she went into the bedroom, saying goodnight, closing the door—and he was alone again.

He could not think of what to do while denying sleep to his body. He had got up late that morning and so was not especially tired. He read the review to the end but politics, the world and other people's artistic and intellectual endeavours hardly interested him now that he himself had embarked on such a momentous project. And so he switched on the television after all and watched the news and a play and an episode in a series of horror stories and then, at midnight, began his vigil, noting his drooping eyelids and heavy limbs until, at half past three in the morning he fell asleep over his desk.

He was asleep for a few minutes: the light of the lamp woke him almost immediately, but again he drowsed off until, with an inkling of the absurdity of the situation, he decided to give up for the evening and go to bed. He went into the bathroom and in his turn brushed his teeth, washed, pissed and then went quietly into the bedroom.

Immediately he sensed that the heavy and fast breathing coming from the bed was unusual. He switched on the lamp and saw that Theresa had kicked all the blankets off her body. She had half-propped herself up in the bed but it was difficult to make out if she was asleep or awake. Her eyes were more or less open but were bleary and unfocused. Her legs and arms kicked and groped weakly as if she was in water: and her breathing was fast, rasping and quite evidently an effort to the mechanism of her body.

Dawson thought at first that she was dreaming. Then he realized that she must be ill. He decided to take her temperature and if it was above normal, call a doctor. He fetched a thermometer from the bathroom and tried to place it in her mouth, but her mouth hung open and the thermometer would not stay in place. Nor could he keep her arm at her side after placing the thermometer in the pit of it. He jogged her and said her name out loud to awaken her, but though sounds came from her mouth, they did not make words that would indicate any consciousness: and all the time her breathing grew faster and more laboured. It seemed as if the lungs or the heart were making intense and frantic effort to perform their functions. Dawson took hold of her wrist to feel her pulse but then, on an inhalation, the breathing stopped. The pulse too had stopped. She was dead.

Dawson woke me at seven that morning by ringing the door bell. I left Arabella in bed and, wearing my pyjamas and dressing-gown, went down to let him in. He had been up all night and looked strange. He told me that Theresa had died, that the doctor had called in the police who had found empty phials of some drug. It was taken to be suicide.

'You're so calm and—I don't know—controlled,' he said. 'I hope you don't mind my coming like this.'

I made some coffee and we sat drinking it. He spoke a lot, saying what had been going through his mind in the past weeks. 'It's my fault, I know, but I didn't mean to.'

'You're sure to feel responsible,' I said. 'One always does in a situation like this. But it's only conceit. We don't have that much effect on one another. If she was going to do it, she would have done it anyway.'

He looked at me but hardly seemed to take in what I said. My phlegmatic consolation did not seem to penetrate to his brain. He left, and I saw him once or twice after that. He gave evidence at the inquest and saw to the funeral—an anonymous affair like their wedding. I tried to get him to come back for a drink afterwards, but he would not, and with no word to me or any one else he left London and disappeared.

Chapter Fourteen

That might have been the end of the story. In the following weeks, one or two people asked after him but by summer he was forgotten. I myself found it difficult to shut him out of my mind. I assumed, of course, that he had either followed Theresa in suicide or had hidden away in a new life that all but obscured his former personality. Both possibilities implied a kind of madness—for there seemed to be no sane way he could go—but whatever course he had chosen, I felt that he should be left alone.

Almost two years after Theresa's death, I went to stay in Scotland with some of my wife's relations. I was angry at myself for allowing her to place me like this in a cold house on barren moorland. The entertainments that had been arranged for us were all *ancien régime*—stalking deer, shooting grouse, billiards, charades and love affairs with each other's wives. I found all the other guests more or less dull, yet was to take two of them back to London in my car—the two turning out to be Henry Poll and Jenny Stanten.

I do not know if those two had come up together (Henry was by now separated from his wife). If that was so, they had fallen out in Scotland, because they slept in separate bedrooms at the hotel in Carlisle. In fact it became clear in the last days of the house-party and on the journey down that Henry Poll was making a play for my wife, Arabella, and she, of course, was reacting favourably to it, if only to punish me for being bored by her cousins.

In Carlisle we stayed at the Grand Hotel and ate an atrocious dinner. After coffee I left the table to buy some cigars at the bar. Jenny came out after me: the other two remained at the table.

'You know,' she said, 'we go very near to Pixhaven to-morrow.'

'What is there there?'

'A Trappist monastery.'

'An old one? Is it worth seeing?'

'Edward's there.'

This was the first time that Dawson had been mentioned between us, or his name spoken at all in my presence for more than a year. I looked at Jenny. Her appearance had not changed, except that the skin around the base of her nose seemed dead and lifeless. Perhaps she had had a cold.

We walked away from the bar. 'Is he a monk, or what?' I asked her.

'Yes. I think he's gone back to being a monk,' she said, 'unless it's some kind of asylum.'

'Not if they're Trappists.' And I remembered what Stendhal said—that Trappists are poor wretches who have not had quite enough courage to kill themselves.

'Don't tell the others.'

'No.'

We came back into the lobby of the hotel. Arabella and Henry were still in the dining-room and had apparently ordered more brandy.

'I want to try and see him,' Jenny said.

'For God's sake . . .' I said, looking into her face. It had an ingenuous expression which seemed unconvincing now that the texture of her skin showed her greater age.

'I must know how he is.'

'Leave him in peace.'

'Do you think he's . . . well . . . off his head?'

'It was a terrible thing to happen—all that, with Theresa. He may well have had a breakdown.'

'But he might have recovered.'

'Yes. And he may still be a broken man.'

I knew that Jenny Stanten's schemes were hard to frustrate,

and her mind was now blatantly working on one. I lit a cigar and walked out into the street. Jenny followed.

'You see, I have to know,' she said.

'What?'

'If he's broken, or mad, or . . . or whatever.'

'Why?'

'I don't know. It's just that if he isn't mad or anything, then he might have learnt something.'

'What?'

'I don't know. Something about life.'

It was late summer. We walked in the greyness and drabness of this northern town—the smell of coal gas and cooling mist in our nostrils. Jenny did not look at me nor I at her.

'He's probably gone back to the Church: certainly, if he's a monk,' I said.

'Yes.'

'One should be grateful, really, if it comforts him—though it was they who mucked him up in the first place.'

'Yes, but that—if he has gone back to the Church like that, for comfort . . . then that would be a kind of breakdown, wouldn't it?'

'Yes. That's what religion is.'

'On the other hand, he might not have done it out of weakness. He might have learnt something, some truth through all the suffering.'

'I doubt it.'

'That's what I have to know.'

'How would you be able to tell?'

'Oh, you could, don't you think? Just from talking to him.'

'Possibly. But you forget that Trappists take a vow of perpetual silence.'

'I know: but the prior is allowed to give a dispensation.'

We came to a small public house on the far side of the station and went into the saloon bar. It was empty. Across it we could see through to a few silent figures drinking beer in the public bar—both men and women, but all old. Jenny sat down at a table and I went to fetch two glasses of whisky.

'You're a Catholic, aren't you?' she asked as I came back to the table.

'I'm as Catholic as you are.'

'But you were at school with him.'

'Yes.'

'And you're a man. It would be easier for you to see him.'

'How did you know he was there?'

'They told me at Kirkham. They knew.'

'You were looking for him?'

'Yes.'

(Silence.)

'Do you still love him?'

'I don't know. It's not that, really. I don't want him back or anything, but I have to know what happened.'

Again we were both silent for a time.

'Why did you leave him?' I asked.

'Oh, you know.' She waved her hand in the air. 'He became so vague and . . . dithering. I thought he was going to turn out just like the others.'

'Did he?'

'I don't know,' she said softly. 'It all depends on what's happened to him now.'

'Yes. I do see.'

When we got back to the hotel, Henry had gone up to his room and Arabella to ours: but I could tell from the look in her eye that something had been set up between them.

We left Carlisle at ten the next morning and were at Pixhaven by half past eleven. The three others dropped me at the priory and drove on to the village a quarter of a mile away. I rang the bell at the door of the monastery and some minutes later the wood behind the grille was pushed back by the hand of a man.

'I should like to speak to the Father Superior,' I said.

The door was opened and I entered a small hallway where the monk, wearing a grey habit, asked me to wait—asked me not with words but with gestures. I sat there for ten or fifteen minutes and then the same monk returned and made signs for me to follow him. I did this—reeling back in my memory to the time of my youth at Kirkham where the sounds and smells had been so much the same.

We went up a flight of stairs and came to a door on which the cleric gave me a measured, gentle knock. He then opened it and led me in. There before me was the prior of Pixhaven whom Dawson had described to me—small, dark, with black bushy hair and spectacles. He rose from his desk and came towards me: I prepared to kiss his ring, to establish, as it were, my credentials as a good son of the Church—but he grasped my hand in a firm, but also measured, clasp and invited me to sit down in a wooden armchair that faced his desk.

'I didn't catch your name,' he said.

'No. I'm sorry. I'm called Robert Winterman.'

'Aha. I'm Anselm Ragg. I'm the prior . . .'

'Yes. It's very good of you to see me like this—without an appointment.'

'Not at all. I have the . . . er . . . responsibility.'

'I've come from London,' I said—and then paused, and then began again—'in the hope of being able to see Father Dawson.'

'I see.'

'I realize that it may not be possible.'

'Yes, well . . . Is he a relation of yours or something like that?'

'A friend. We were both at school at Kirkham.'

'Are you a journalist?'

'Yes, but . . .'

'I remember now that he once mentioned you.'

'We were friends.'

'Yes.'

'And I've come to realize that I really rather depend on him.'

'In what sense?'

'Well . . . spiritually. For advice.'

'You haven't seen him for two years or so?'

'No. That's just it.'

'Have you no other spiritual adviser?'

'No.'

'Isn't it a mistake to depend on a single—and rather changeable—person like that?'

'Well, it may be, but we've been through so much of our life together. Our youth . . . and afterwards.'

The prior looked down at his hands. 'He has taken a vow of perpetual silence, you know.'

'Yes. I know that.'

'It is possible to grant a dispensation, but I mustn't do it lightly.'

'I wouldn't ask, if it weren't for the sake of my soul.'

The prior stood up. 'If you wait here, I'll ask him.' Then he turned to face me. 'He's been through a lot, as you say: on the other hand . . .'

I was left alone in this study, so like the rooms at the monks at Kirkham. The polish. The bare floor. The ugly crucifix on the wall. An environment purged of beauty and humanity, obsessed only with perverting nature in the name of supernatural law. A rare rage passed through me. What could they have done to Dawson now, when they had already destroyed his life? What kind of broken man was I to see? What species of lunacy? What variety of despair? I was not surprised that they were going to let me see him. I knew the arrogance of these clerics. The prior would be itching to test his cure: to see if the runaway slave was now adequately fettered—and all in the name of free will and moral choice. What cunning there is in men who invent dogmas that make falsehood seem truth.

The prior returned. He crossed to the window of his room and pointed out towards the hills. 'Do you see the farm?' he said. 'There, the yard? You'll find your friend over there.'

Like a pious and obedient Catholic, I thanked the prior and then went out of his room and down the stairs and out on to the lawn behind the monastery. The farm was separated from the cloistered area by a stone wall, but there was a small gate between the two and I made for that. I passed through it and crossed to the fold-yard where four men were loading manure on to a cart. I could not see at once if any one of them was Dawson: but a young man with close-cropped hair noticed that I was watching them and made a sign to someone the other side of the trailer. This man came into sight. It was Dawson. He recognized me and lifted his hand and gave a vague wave of greeting. He too had short hair and wore grey overalls like the others. His face had become exceedingly thin, thin though it had always been; and if I had not known otherwise, I would have said that he was ten years older than I was.

He came out of the fold-yard and took my arm, leading me through the small gate back on to the monastery lawn. We walked together towards the wooden fence at the foot of the lawn which separated it from the rough grass that ran up to the escarpment above us. I followed him in climbing over this fence, and together we walked up the hill. The sky was white, the sun's illumination diffuse, casting no shadow.

He said nothing and I could not bring myself to break the silence. I felt anxious and looked to see the expression on his face. There was none—or perhaps a faint smile. I felt within myself a strange combination of respect and embarrassment. Perhaps it was because he seemed so much older: or maybe I felt ashamed of the spurious curiosity that had brought me here.

We reached a point on the hill where the grass ended and the shale began. Here Dawson sat down and I sat down a few feet from him. He looked into my eyes but I had no question to ask him: therefore he spoke.

He explained how he had regained his faith and had come here to Pixhaven. He described the life they led—the prayer, meditation, labour and asceticism. I questioned him on the value of this life, and he spoke of the soul and of God as though the soul was the only facet of his identity and God the only person of any account. So then I reminded him of his fellow men—their suffering, their oppression. He nodded. He explained that a monk, though outside society, still prayed to God on behalf of mankind: that this communication with our creator could not be measured on a utilitarian scale of values. He said he thought that there was great confusion in our generation between social and religious morality—between the exigencies of human life and the deference that was due to God.

He spoke with such unhesitating authority that I looked into his eyes for signs of conceit: but there was none. They were fixed, almost in a squint, on some point in the middle-distant space. His tone of voice was strange, measured but unhesitating. There was an economy and exactness in the formation of each phrase, as if he was speaking an alien tongue that he had learnt from the reading of its literature.

I asked him how he could be so sure that his beliefs were true. He then described the state of absolute concentration that he had reached through meditation and self-denial, where the truth of a proposition may be measured by the physical sensation of ecstasy and release that it provokes in the brain and spine, I questioned him more closely on the nature of this feeling: he said that there were intimations of it in a yawn or a laugh. He said it must be like that which brings a moth out of darkness towards the brightest light.

And then, for a moment, my respect gave way to irritation at his certainty. I told him who it was who was waiting for me in the village of Pixhaven. He nodded and asked after her, but with only the most cursory interest. I then asked him if Theresa, having killed herself, was now in Hell. That did provoke, perhaps, an expression of slight pain—though expressions are sometimes hard to interpret. God had had mercy on him, he said, and he would surely have had mercy on her, since she was more deserving.

I then felt remorse at having asked such a question. I said that he knew me and the kind of life I led, and asked him if it was evil. He said he could not judge, but that though body and mind might confuse my soul with defences and excuses for the way in which I lived, nevertheless my conscience could not be destroyed. I might refuse to call evil by that name, but certain acts and patterns of behaviour would be manifestly undignified, contradicting the tight logic of my being with negative and destructive patterns of thought and behaviour. One did not attain a state of grace through a continuous succession of right actions, but by the understanding of the contradictions within oneself, a containment of them and hence the preservation of one's moral integrity. Sin was inevitable, but there was an antidote in repentance. Evil was that pride which denied the contradiction.

The sky remained white. There was no sign of the passing of time. The curve of the lake shore below us, the squares of the buildings and the lines of the stone walls that ran up the side of the green hills, all became a placid, abstract pattern whose repose permitted a stillness of mind. We talked further, and then for moments there was silence and the silence took on a value equal to the speech. It was a peaceful part of England: but I knew that there were others waiting for me, so I stood to go.

Dawson walked with me down the hill and offered to take me out through their church. We entered it through a small door that opened on to the lawn. At this level there was a crypt with six altars where, he explained, the monks would say mass in the morning. Then we climbed a narrow spiral staircase to the choir above—its stalls without misericords. Behind the altar was a metal grille which shut off that part of the nave used by the lay Catholics of the locality: but cut into the grille was a small gate through which the celebrant of the mass could pass with the Eucharist. Through this door, Dawson explained, I could find my way out of the monastery.

I asked him how much of each day he spent in the church. Six hours, it seems, were spent singing the *Opus Dei*. He looked at the choir and altar with obvious affection. Was he happy, then, I asked. He did not answer. He sometimes felt impatient at night, he said, because sleep was surely a waste of time. I said what I thought was expected—that I envied him his faith and certainty. He said he would pray for me.

We shook hands and I left him, passing through the grille into the other part of the church. I closed the gate, but then turned because I had meant to ask him his name—his monastic name—whether it was now John or Edward or something else. But through the grille I could see him kneeling at his place in the choir. I felt I should not interrupt him, so I turned again and went out into the open air. The three others were in the pub in the village. They sat with empty glasses and plates on the table next to them. Henry Poll and Arabella were irritated at having had to wait for so long.

'Who the devil was he, this friend of yours?' Henry Poll asked me.

'Someone I knew at school,' I replied.

I went to the bar and bought a pork pie, and then suggested that we should drive on if we were to get back to London that night.

I sat in the driver's seat of the car and Jenny sat next to me.

Henry and Arabella seemed happy to be on the back seat. As I adjusted the mirror, I could see that the fingers of his right hand were in the cleft beneath her left knee.

Jenny said nothing as we drove out of Pixhaven, but I felt her eyes on my face and became confused, not knowing what expression to give to it. But then, a mile or two further on, Henry and Arabella started to talk about food in country pubs and Jenny leant closer to me and asked, in a low voice, how he had been.

'A bit thinner,' I said, 'but quite well.'

'Yes, but was he happy?'

'He seemed happy, yes. Calm, at any rate.'

She sat back and was quiet for a few minutes: then she leant forward again. 'What did you think, though?'

'How do you mean?'

'Was he mad or sane?'

'He wasn't mad. Not at all.'

'But broken?'

'I don't know. It depends.'

'On what?'

'I don't know . . . on whether you believe in God or not.'

'Then he was sick.'

'Why?'

'Because you don't believe in God.'

'That's true.'

She broke out of her quiet voice into a quick, sharp manner. 'You don't, do you? You never did. It's a defence. An illusion. He was a fool.'

'Perhaps.'

'Not perhaps. Definitely. You said . . . you said it was the school that had buggered him up.'

'I said that. Yes.'

'And you still think that, don't you?'

'I suppose so. But now he seemed . . . I don't know . . . so much at ease with himself.'

Then Jenny sat back and was silent and started to chew the inside of her cheek.

'Who are you talking about?' Arabella asked from the back seat.

I looked at Jenny to see if she would reply, but she was intent on gnawing the knuckle of her thumb—her head bent forward, her eyes staring at her own knees.

'Monk Dawson,' I said.

Piers Paul Read
The Junkers 80p

A young British diplomat in West Berlin has a passionate
affair with Suzi, a beautiful German girl, while engaged in an
undercover investigation into powerful men in today's
prosperous Germany – men who may be ex-Nazi war criminals.
As he digs deeper, he uncovers an appalling catalogue of
murders and sexual atrocities ...

'Dazzling writing ... almost a panoramic view of history'
FINANCIAL TIMES

Alive 95p

There were 16 survivors. Despaired of by their families, they
had survived against all odds a plane crash and ten long weeks
of endurance in the icy, desolate wastes of the Andes
mountains. Piers Paul Read was chosen by these young men to
tell, quite unsparingly, their story : a story of constant faith,
unbounded determination and immense courage – and of how
they broke the greatest taboo of mankind ...

'One of the classic survival stories of all time' DAILY MAIL

Polonaise 95p

Count Stefan Kornowski, born in 1914 on his father's Polish
country estate, is destined for the comfortable, if limited, life
of the Catholic aristocracy. By the time he is fifteen, his mother
has died, his sister has been seduced, his father has been declared
bankrupt and gone mad ... This rich and complex novel traces the
fortunes of the Kornowski family through the troubled, mid-
century years as they face crises of family, faith and political
involvement which lead from Warsaw to a country house in
Cornwall.

Wilbur Smith
A Sparrow Falls £1.25

From the trenches of France in the First World War, through
the violence of the Johannesburg strikes of the 1920s the last
chapter of Sean Courtney's epic life takes him home to the serene
splendours of the African wilderness.

'A man's world, where hate can swell like biceps and frontiers
beckon as seductively as a woman . . . Wilbur Smith writes as
forcefully as his tough characters act'

Gerald Green
The Hostage Heart 80p

One of the world's richest and most powerful men lies on the
operating table, undergoing complex arterial surgery. Behind the
surgeon stands a man with a gun. He is a revolutionary terrorist,
fanatical and meglomaniac. The terrorist group is demanding ten
million dollars in two hours. Their hostage lies unconscious within
a hairsbreadth of death. . .

Colin Dexter
The Silent World of Nicholas Quinn 75p

The newly appointed member of the Oxford Examinations
Syndicate was deaf, provinical and gifted. Now he's dead. The
trail leads Inspector Morse into a murder puzzle where the clues
include an assortment of unsavoury academics, the Arab
connections who provide the Syndicates and two tasty ladies ; . .
And then there's the second murder at the Syndicate . . .

' . . . superior, meticuously-plotted classical detective story'
GUARDIAN

Jack Bickham
Twister 80p

Twister is a tornado – the most devastating force ever to emerge
from the world of the elements . . . it moves across America
leaving a trail of devastation and death . . . no life touched by
the Twister, as it wreaks a billion dollars worth of damage, will
ever be the same again . . .

'Blends fact and fiction in a tale that will chill'
PUBLISHERS WEEKLY

Kit Thackeray
Crownbird 70p

Four men and one woman with a plan to change the face of
Africa . . . where the stranglehold of the Chinese is daily more
threatening . . . Their mission – on orders from Whitehall – is
an 'adjustment', violent if necessary, of the power politics of
the Dark Continent.

Newton Thornburg
Cutter and Bone 80p

Cutter – a mangled veteran of Vietnam, a cripple who's two
parts crazy. Bone – a drop-out from the executive big-time,
a parasite misfit and professional womanizer. Together they're
bound for the Ozark hills in pursuit of a country-boy tycoon who
might just be the killer of a teenage prostitute.

'Crazy, superlative . . . a weird and fascinating trip'
LOS ANGELES TIMES

Elmore Leonard
Unknown Man No. 89 80p

The man handed him a hundred and fifty bucks and a name.
All Ryan had to do was to find the guy who wears the name.
The tracing job took him right through the seamy side of Detroit
city — hoodlums in leather jackets, a cop who wears long hair
and a Magnum under his jacket, a girl who's drinking her way
to hell in a wine bottle and only stopping off for sex . . .

'A gritty American teaser . . .' DAILY MIRROR

Zeno
The Four Sergeants 75p

Sicily 1943 : A sabotage operation behind enemy lines, to blow a
bridge behind a Panzer Division and smash Axis withdrawal
strategy. The men — a hand-picked Airborne platoon — include a
section of German Jews . . . soldiers who can never allow
themselves to be taken alive . . .

'In the war yarn class, this book rates high . . . tense, authentic'
SUNDAY TELEGRAPH

Samuel Edwards
All That Glitters 75p

An urgent cablegram from the Chinese wife he hasn't seen
in years takes a top New York surgeon into Hong Kong's exotic
world of glitter and squalor — and involves him in a terrifying web
of gold and smuggling, crime and sudden death . . .

'An all-action thriller' MANCHESTER EVENING NEWS